Turing to the Death
and other stories

by Robert Kibble

1995

Table of Contents

The Amazing Cause-And-Effect Man

The little red lights on the jukebox in the corner finally changed. CD 23 track 4. At last, Sarah thought to herself. She had waited almost an hour for it already in a bar she didn't like and didn't normally consider. It was one of the weird pubs with wooden barrels on their sides for tables and uncomfortable stools scattered around. Supposedly the beer was amazing, but Sarah only drank Guinness, and that was mediocre at best.

All I wanna do is have a little fun before I die, says a man next to me out of nowhere, apropos of nothing he says him name is William...

"My name is William, you know." She hadn't even seen him arrive, let alone pull up a stool next to her. He wore black jeans and a plain grey tee-shirt, the colour suggesting it used to be black but had faded from too many washes. He had a slight smile on his pockmarked face, as if he knew her already and was enjoying watching her guess. Sarah frowned at him for a few seconds, and then decided he was just a student-type trying to chat her up. She nodded at him and returned to her Guinness, hoping he would go away. Either that or the barmaid would turn up the jukebox a bit so she could hear the song anyway.

...and he's plain ugly to me, and I wonder if he's ever had a day of fun...

"Sorry to have troubled you," he said, and threw a glass of

whiskey down his throat. "It's just I thought you might not want to die today." He placed the glass gently back on the bar, then stood up and pulled his coat off the bar-stool where he had slung it earlier. Sarah looked down, wondering how long he'd been there. She couldn't have been paying attention.

"It that a threat?" she asked, still angry that the guy was interrupting her listening.

Even that level of interest seemed to be taken as an invitation, and he hung the coat back on the bar-stool and sat down again, waving a finger at the bar-maid. "No, it's a statement of my own opinion. I thought you might not want to die. That is all."

She couldn't hear the song, and there seemed little point in trying. It was a stupid idea to put it on anyway. It would only remind her of the weekend. It was hearing that song that had made her feel courageous enough to visit her parents, and look where that had got her. She'd even had a row with her flatmate, Jo. She looked up at the man again. He was staring straight into her eyes, unblinking. "Look," she said. "If this is a weird attempt at a chat-up by trying to confuse me, it's not going to work. I'm not interested."

"Let me assure you, Sarah, that I have no physical interest in you whatsoever." She would have found that rather hurtful if she wasn't trying to work out where he could have found out her name from. "I am merely trying to determine if you would like my help in surviving the day."

"So just how am I going to die then? And how did you know my name?" She avoided looking directly at him, finding it extremely disconcerting that she hadn't seen him blink yet.

"Your manner of death is largely up to you. There are many

futures open to us from here. And as to how I know your name, I just know. I also know that the reason you are here today is because of your mother shouting at you last week for not wearing your good dress to the interview."

"What? I'm here because I wanted a drink." The echoes of the arguments of the last two days had been ringing round her head all morning. She needed a drink.

"JD again please," he said, turning to the barmaid who had just appeared behind his left shoulder. He turned and threw a twenty-pound note onto the bar. "And whatever this young lady is drinking. And have one yourself. You look as if you need it."

The barmaid looked over at Sarah. "Not for me thanks," Sarah replied.

"Sure?" he asked.

"Positive."

"That'll be three-seventeen, then," said the barmaid, putting a shot-glass down on the bar. A moment later she placed two notes and some change next to it.

"It is a tragedy, it really is."

"What?" asked Sarah, irritated that her song would be finishing in a minute and she'd hardly heard any of it.

"The barmaid, Clare. She will... oh well, it isn't important. Not to you."

"Like you know what's important to me."

"Your mother's approval is."

"Well there's a great piece of psychic power. You look at someone and say 'Your mother is very important in your life.' Or 'was' if she turns out to be dead. It's like saying 'You don't want to die'. Oh, but of course, you said that, too."

"Your mother shouted at you for not putting on the dress, which made you go back and throw the dress around your bedroom at home and then left it on the floor, which meant that when you spilled the coffee down the side of the bed it stained the dress, which meant you had to bring it in to get it dry-cleaned, which is why you are here today waiting until it is ready to be picked up."

"How the hell did you know that?"

"I saw you."

"You some kind of stalker or something?"

"No." He looked upwards. "I just see the way the world fits together. That's all. You have reached a decision point. From here there are many ways the world can go, and it is your decision."

"Oh, right, like chaos. I saw *Jurassic Park*, too, you know."

"No, not like chaos. Chaos is unpredictability, minute changes having dramatic and unforeseen consequences. This is not like that at all. Once this decision is made, the world will fall into one of the patterns I can see, and once there it will remain."

"Right, so my life is going to be totally changed by picking up a dress. Like the barmaid's life will be changed by you buying her a drink."

He looked round at the barmaid, who was putting some glasses into the dishwasher. "No, that has made no difference. She will die tonight. She will be run over on her way home." For a brief moment his eyes seemed to glaze over, as if he was looking at something behind the bar.

"So tell her, and maybe she'll get a taxi," Sarah suggested.

"No," he replied, turning back to Sarah. "Her life is over. There will be no more decisions."

"Oh great, so it's only me you're interested in. How come I get the nutters? So I suppose something terrible is waiting for me if I just get up and leave, right?"

"That depends. If you walk out and collect your dress now, you will get home in time for *Dr Zhivago*, and you'll settle down in front of the TV. When it starts getting a bit colder you'll turn the gas fire on, and then fall asleep fifteen minutes before the end like you did last time. The gas fire has begun leaking, and you will never wake up. It is not an unpleasant death, but I suspect you would still dislike the prospect."

Something in the tone of his voice made her shiver slightly. It was as if he was saying something so obvious it was impossible for her to deny it.

"So I don't turn the fire on."

"Of course you don't. Not now. You won't get home if you leave now, because a young man will be in the dry-cleaner's already. He will have lost his ticket and you will have to wait almost twenty minutes. When you leave it will be getting dark, and you will take the short-cut across the ford to get home in time for the film. You will never see the man who hits you. There will be a lot of pain, but it will be mercifully brief."

Sarah's hands had started shaking. The man's face seemed odd now, too. There had been no change, not really, but his eyes were staring at her as if it were a matter of life-and-death. She kept trying to tell herself that he was mad, or she was mad, but he spoke so clearly and with such force that she found it impossible not to believe what he was saying.

"So when do I have to leave?" she asked, all sarcasm gone from her voice.

"Closing time," he replied. "You will leave at closing time. You will end up spending the night at someone else's house, although you will not sleep. Tomorrow morning you will arrive home to the slight smell of gas, and will report it immediately."

"I will," she said, still shaking. She swallowed the last of her pint and looked over at the barmaid.

"Good. Would you like that drink now, then?"

She accepted, and he bought her another pint. When she had finished it, he bought yet another one. They sat in silence at the bar, him staring down into his whiskeys and her staring towards her own reflection in the mirror below the optics. She didn't want to die. That was all she could think of. Her eyes were wide open, and she could hardly blink. She didn't want to die.

Just as the barmaid came to throw the two of them out, the man picked up his coat and walked quickly out of the pub. Sarah got up and ran after him, wanting to thank him. She pushed the door open, only to see him running across the road away from her. She thought about calling after him, but realised she didn't know his name.

On the other side of the road he joined a group of young men and one woman. Sarah glanced at her once, and then looked again. Jo. What was her flatmate doing here...? She took a step forwards. Then, in an instant, she realised. As a ten-pound note changed hands, Sarah just stopped, dead, wanting to be somewhere else. Wanting to have gone to a different pub, or not listened to him. Anything rather than standing in the road, all of them laughing at her, staring at her. She shut her eyes, trying to make sure she didn't cry.

Jo of all people. They were friends. How could she...?

Sarah turned to run.

The car seemed to come from nowhere.

It swerved away from her with a screech and collided with a lamp-post. She turned instinctively, and saw it recoil sideways from the lamp-post, sliding towards the bar entrance. The barmaid was just leaving, and stood, stock-still, staring at the car coming towards her. Sarah tried to shout, but no sound came out. Someone screamed.

The car smashed into the front wall of the pub. The barmaid looked like a crash test dummy as she was crushed between car and wall. Her eyes were still wide open after the car had ricocheted off the wall. She stood upright for almost a second before falling to the pavement.

When the car stopped the boys were silent, and the note had been dropped. Sarah looked down at her hands - they had stopped shaking. She looked over at the group, standing around, pointedly not looking at each other. The man was staring towards the accident, as afraid as she had been a few minutes before.

Sarah crossed the road, slowly walking towards him. She smiled as she approached. He began to back off.

"Thank you," she said, picking up the note and handing it back to him. "Take it. You deserve it."

He held out his hand. It was shaking violently, and he dropped the note almost instantly. "Oh my God," he said, stuttering.

"You thought you were making it up, didn't you?"

He didn't move.

"Can you see the future now?" she asked, quietly. "Are you going to tell all of these people their futures?" She waved her hand towards the group. Jo was looking at her, tears streaming down her face.

He continued staring at the stationary car, as motionless as the scene in front of him. He wasn't even breathing.

Sarah nodded. She took out her diary. After making a note to check for a gas-leak tomorrow, she settled down to wait for the police.

Alone in the Electric Chair

I feel tired more than anything.

Tired of the struggle, of trying to be, to live in this world.

I am only dimly aware of the people in front of me, watching me, hating me for my very existence. They do not understand, but who am I to ask them to? I do not understand.

It was late at night, and I was tired. Tired then as I am tired now, but for different reasons. I had been busy that day, working late and driving home. My wife was waiting for me, waiting to attack me for tardiness, or untidiness, or any one of a number of things she attacked me for.

The strap is cutting into my wrist. I wish they could have tied it a little looser. I wouldn't be able to move much anyway, but the pain is irritating. It's stupid that I care, though.

There is a flash of light behind me, reflected in the window opposite. It obscures the faces behind for a moment, giving me relief from the staring. A blue light. I remember a blue flashing light, from the time they found me.

My wife was dead. Lying next to me, blood still flooding out of her body.

I watched as they walked round the car, terrified of what they saw. They looked into my eyes then as the starers do now. None of them understood what I felt then, nor what I feel now.

Their eyes are burning into me, making my cheeks feel hot. Why should I be ashamed or remorseful? What's done is done, right? I can't change the past now, much as I might want to.

They took me away and I never got to see her body again. They didn't even let me see her before she was cremated. They thought it would be too dangerous.

So here I am. My life is over.

They are still watching me, though. I have their attention. For another few minutes anyway. Then they'll wander off, slightly quiet, wondering what to say. They'll start the conversation with some bland remark about the weather, ignoring me completely. They don't want to know about people like me.

I can't face any more of it. The cars I hear remind me of that night, just as the faces I see remind me of her. Maybe I regret it after all. Maybe I want it all to be different. Of course I do, but it doesn't help. It's over for me.

I push the joystick forwards. The electric motor bursts into life as I head for home. I can't face the city centre today.

Three Cages, However Gilded

Between the final heartbeat and the moment of death there is almost a second when the heart is still waiting to beat again. There may be up to five or so when the brain has not realised what is happening. That depends on the person. Some who have come close to death see their lives flash in front of them. Some see a tunnel stretching upwards. Some see darkness approaching.

Possibly the type of near-death experience depends on the person. Perhaps a life flashing in front of the eyes is the mind's way of keeping itself together. Perhaps the tunnel represents a future so strong that death is no yet an option. Perhaps the darkness is a sign of the horror of oblivion, and the shock is enough to throw the mind back into the body.

Sometimes there is a combination of all three.

The stretcher was lifted into the ambulance, the drip already attached to the young man - the only survivor so far. The paramedics said nothing. They sat opposite each other, occasionally shaking their heads.

There's a Ford in front of me, like the company car I used to own, only with one of those flaps on the back. Left there's a Rover, with a number-plate you can make the word ANKH out of. And there are those two lorries up ahead, the dirty white one trying to overtake uphill. It isn't managing. Why can't it just fall back and let me past? It's holding everyone up. And the right lane is whizzing past. There's a gap coming up. Just ahead of that red car. The brown one goes past. I drop back to allow space between me and the Ford in front. The blue car goes past. I speed up, ready to move into the right lane. Then the second blue car. I begin to pull out.

15

Suddenly the brake lights on the Ford in front light up. I'm looking right, and don't see it straight away. It's closing far too fast. I swerve right, slamming my foot on the brakes. There's a loud noise and my seatbelt is cutting into my shoulder. Then another noise. This time I feel heavy, pushed back into the seat. I see a Citroen going past left to right. There's another car to my right, almost stationary.

I see the coach coming.

Dr Anderson always hated ringing the relatives, but he never felt he could ask a nurse to do it. At least this time the parents would have a chance to get here while their son was still alive. He paused part-way through the dialling. No matter how many people he saw die, it never stopped hurting. Some of his colleagues made light of it, some even made jokes about patients dying all the time. It was at times like this that he wondered if he was cut out for this job.

The coach appears again. Just to my right. I can see it slowing down, but not fast enough. Nowhere near fast enough. I want it to swerve, to hit one of the lorries, but it keeps coming. It hits the red car first. The red car leaves the ground and flies over the central reservation. Another car collides with it. And another. The first car to collide is already crushed into half its size. I can see the man inside staring across at me. Straight at me.

The doctor arrived back in the theatre just in time to see Pete's body begin shaking violently. "Hasn't he been anaesthetised yet?" he shouted.

The anaesthetist was on the other side of the table. "As much as we can give him, doctor. I can't give him any more. His muscles shouldn't be able to move."

His chest pushed up slightly, his back clearing the table for a second before the nurse pushed it back down again. Dr Anderson turned and shouted for one of the orderlies. "Get some straps. We can't perform an operation like this!"

"But he's conscious!" shouted one of the nurses. Dr Anderson looked up at the EEG machine. True enough. There was a lot of activity there.

"If we don't operate he'll die. I don't care if he's conscious or not."

The orderly arrived back with the straps, and helped strap Pete down to the table. Once the straps were in place, Pete stopped trying to move at all. The activity on the EEG machine died down, too.

The coach smashes into the side of my car, throwing me up into the air. I can see children inside being thrown forwards. One had been walking along the aisle, and flies straight into the windscreen. The windscreen shatters, and the child's head hangs out. Her eyes are still open despite the blood pouring down her face. She looks down at me, and narrows her eyes.

"His heart's stopped!"

The nurse had already wheeled forwards the defibrillator, and was rubbing the two plates together.

"Now," said Dr Anderson, pulling his knife back away from the body in case it managed to break out of the straps.

The nurse held the plates down on the chest, and the body shook violently. There was a single peak on the monitor, then nothing.

"Again."

Another burst, and another peak. And another. The heart continued, albeit faintly. Dr Anderson breathed a sigh of relief and returned to the surgery.

Looking up, I see the coach driver slumped forwards in his seat. His head is hanging strangely, too far to the left. There is a small piece of glass embedded in his head. As I stare at him he opens his eyes and tries to say something. He is speaking slowly, but I cannot make it out. Then I realise I cannot hear anything. He stops talking, and just stares at me. I see his eyes fading. They close again, despite his efforts to remain conscious.

All around me is silent. As I look around, I see their faces looking at me. My car is undamaged. I get out, and look around again. The man over the reservation. The driver. The child smashed against the windscreen. A mother and baby thrown forwards in another car. Another passenger on the coach. One of the lorry drivers whose lorry turned over. They all stare back at me. They all begin moving towards me. As they form a circle I count them. Seventeen. All staring.

The circle breaks. The people step aside, and the landscape fades away. There is a building - no, a terrace of houses. I look to the sides and see the street stretching off into the distance on both sides. Behind me is a row of shops.

One of the doors stands open. I walk towards it, taking three steps up into the perfectly-maintained garden, up to the red front door, with the hanging light above it.

I walk through. There is no smell, nor motion of the air. Even the door seems to swing without disturbing its environment. There is no sound. One of the interior doors stands open, with light streaming out from within. I walk towards it and look through. The door swings open in front of me.

There is a young man sitting staring up at the ceiling. He has a glass of whiskey and ice in his left hand, resting on the arm of the chair. There are red lines from his eyes down to the corners of his mouth. There is a bottle on the other side of the chair, mostly finished.

The old man who was pointing at me walks up behind me.

"What is going on?" I ask.

He does not answer. Instead, by way of answering, he points to the far corner of the room. There is an upright piano, on top of which is a yellowed black-and-white photograph of a woman. A pretty girl, with wide dark eyes and a narrow face.

"Who was she?"

"Our friend's sister. She died over a hundred years ago."

"But he is still young. He is still alive."

"If you call this living, then yes, he is. He spends each day the same, drinking himself into trying to forget, although he never does. Is that living?"

I look down at the man again. He shakes his head, and takes another sip. His hand is shaking.

"But he is alive. He could change."

"Not now. What keeps him alive is his love for her, or his hatred of the world that allowed her to die. If he comes to terms with her death, he will die as well."

"Why doesn't he do that, then?"

"Because he couldn't stand to let the last memory of her die. He believes part of her lives on in him. He doesn't believe his torments should ever end."

"How do you know?"

"Because I have seen death, my friend. And now I have lived it. I have known the tragedy. It gets a little easier every day, but it never goes away. No matter how long you live, it is always there, waiting for you. One day you will see something that reminds you, and it will all come back as if it had never gone away. For him the tragedy is so great, so all-consuming, that there is never a moment of peace. Each second brings back more memories, and each moment is worse than the last. If you live long enough and you care at all, this fate is inevitable."

The room goes dark, and I close my eyes.

Pete's mother ran through the hospital towards the theatre. A nurse stopped her outside the room itself. "What's happening?" she screamed.

The nurse turned her round gently and led her over to a seat. "You are Mrs Dawson?"

She nodded.

"Your son is in a critical condition. He was in a bad motorway accident. We will let you know as soon as anything happens."

"I want to see him."

"I'm afraid that's not possible at the moment. The doctor is operating now."

"Why? What's happening?"

"A piece of the steering wheel was lodged in his lung, a few inches down from his heart. The doctor is trying to remove it."

The nurse put an arm round her, wondering how long she could spare before she had to get back to her work.

I am in the circle once again. There are only sixteen now, though. One young girl walks forwards. She is something like fourteen. Could be as old as eighteen. I never was any good at judging ages. She has long blond hair, parted in the middle. Her mouth is hanging slightly open, and she is not looking at me, but at something over my right shoulder.

"Why did you kill me?"

I stand there, staring at her. What can I say? What does she

21

want me to say? I'm sorry? I don't even know her. Sorry can't bring her back, but I say I'm sorry anyway.

"Sorry. You are sorry."

"Yes. I'm very sorry. It was an accident."

"I am dead. I was fifteen. I was good at school, and went out and had fun on Friday nights, and never had sex with my boyfriend, and now I never will. You took my life away from me. What are you going to give me back?"

"I have nothing to give."

"Your life. You killed us. You don't deserve to live."

"But I didn't mean to..."

The voices of the others join in, all in chorus. "You don't deserve to live... Die..."

I stand there, watching the circle closing in around me. The truck driver, and the mother carrying her baby, and the children. All closing in, all chanting. I can't feel anything.

Then, suddenly, the circle parts again. The dead baby is standing there, upright as any adult. "You lied to her," it says with an adult male voice.

"What?" I look at the girl, still standing there. "How?"

"You could give her something. You could give her a life back. You could give us all life."

"How?"

"Show her the path back."

"What path?"

"The path. The one you took." His voice is malicious, as if he believes I am hiding something, as if I am lying.

"I don't know what you're talking about."

"Maybe not." His voice is nicer, now. Kind and quiet. The others are staring down at the ground, seemingly ashamed of being near him. "Let me show you another life. Pick me up."

I lean down and lift him. Instinctively I put him over my right shoulder, looking back, the way I carry my friend's child when I visit. "So I can see, idiot," he says. I turn him round so he faces forwards. "Walk."

The circle is stripped away, and the ground changes. There is now a small wooden shack in the middle of a beautiful landscape. There are mountains in the background, and a waterfall, and pines. It is perfect.

The shack rushes towards us. No, towards me. I look down at my arms, but the baby has gone. As the shack approaches, I see the dead girl from the circle standing inside. Another man is inside, cleaning blood off his hands. There is another young girl, one who looks a bit like the dead one. She is covered with blood, lying on the floor. Her hands are tied to the legs of a large wooden table. She looks very thin. I look at the man and feel like vomiting.

"You find this path distasteful?" asks the girl as I approach.

"Has he just...?" I ask, more for some sign of why I am being shown this than confirmation of the obvious.

"Yes. What else can he do?"

"What? He's just killed that girl..."

"Yes. He killed her, because it is all he has left. Each death is different, each one unique. He enjoys them. He keeps them here for weeks sometimes, toying with them."

"Why don't you call the police?"

She laughs. "I am dead, remember? And anyway, what could they do? They would execute him, as they have done before, and then he would return. His fire still burns, and always will. He lives for the moment of the kill, now, and knows he need fear no execution."

"So what can we do to stop him?"

"You can't. He made his choice. And he will survive whatever you do to stop him."

"That's horrible."

"Indeed it is. But that is the end point of hedonism."

"That isn't just hedonism! He just tortured and killed a girl..."

"...and you think that's 'inhuman'. He's a monster, perhaps. No. He was perfectly normal once. He loved, and he enjoyed his life. He was very popular, and widely considered a good man. Women flocked to him, and he loved each one of them with a passion and tenderness almost unknown in the time. With each one he found new ways to please them and himself. And then he was found guilty of adultery during one of humanity's drives towards justice. He was hanged."

"So why isn't he dead?"

The girl shakes her head. "You still don't see, do you? His fire brought him back, held him in this world even though his body was gone. He returned and resumed the life he had left. As the centuries past, he went further and further. This is just an extension. It is his only escape from boredom. He deludes himself that the girls enjoy it. He does not believe he does anything wrong."

A door slams behind us. It is dark. Her voice is deeper, now. "Show me the path. Let my fire burn again."

Dr Anderson begins to cut, trying at first to find out how much damage the steering wheel has caused. Far too much is his first reaction. This man should already be dead. Then he sighs. And probably will die, whatever I do, comes the reply from inside.

He glances up at the machines and pauses for an instant. If there were any other survivors of the accident, he'd be operating on them instead. As he begins, he tries to shake off the feeling that this is a futile waste of time. Then he remembers the mother sitting outside, her whole life now revolving around this man lying in front of him.

He begins to remove the wheel, already bent out of shape by the man's rigid hands during the accident. For the next few minutes, he does not even pause for breath.

The circle forms again, and again I stand within, staring at its representative this time. A middle-aged man, just beginning to lose some of his hair. He walks forwards.

"I'm sorry," I begin. He interrupts me.

"All my life I've worked and worked, and saved every penny I could, and I did well for myself. Set myself up with a nice pension, and nearly own my own house, and you do that stupid manoeuvre of yours and it's all over. All my life working, and you..."

He stops. Another man, mid-fifties but well-dressed walks into the circle. He waves a hand, and the others all disappear.

"You know what you are becoming, don't you?"

"Am I like those two they showed me?"

"Either like one of them, or like the third. The one I will show you."

"So who's the third. Where are we going now."

"Nowhere. You're looking at him."

"So what's your story?"

"I am on the board of a group of companies, earning three hundred thousand a year. Last year I had thirty-four girlfriends, ranging from seventeen to thirty-eight, and I'm over fifty."

"So what's the problem?"

He thinks for a moment. "Oh no, my mistake. That's next year."

"What?"

"It's next year I'll be having all that. I remember now. This

26

year I was just preparing for it all, working hard."

"So who are you now?"

"I'm an office clerk. But they'll promote me soon. I'll get there."

"What? What about the girlfriends?"

"Oh, that'll come with the job. I'll start going out and getting them once I've got the job sorted. It won't take long, just a few more months and they'll realise how hard I'm working for them."

"You're mad!"

"No, Peter. You are. I am just like you. What you dream of now you will always dream of. I am what you are, and you will never be more. Give up now, accept your death. You have no future."

"I have every future. Just because you failed..."

"Means you will. You will always dream for more, dream to be more. Dream to be something you are not yet, but think you might be sometime in the future. And you will have forever to try for it."

"So I'll manage sooner or later."

"No you won't. You'll put off the real changes. Without a death to drive home the perspective of life you will fail. Forever. You will always want more. You have ambition, Peter, and that does not sit well with eternity."

The darkness closes in again.

Pete felt very faint. There were people around him, some of
them crying. They believed he was dying. He knew that, but
didn't know how. He felt his heart beating weakly. Thump.
Thump. Then a pause.

*The baby was sitting opposite me in a high-chair, playing with
a piece of banana. The blood running down its forehead did
not seem to be bothering it half as much as the piece of skin it
had just dropped onto the floor.*

"Fetch it for me, would you?" it asks.

I lean down and pick it up. "So what now?"

*"You choose. You have taken the path, but you can still choose.
Give up now and accept, and you will die. The other way
depends on the path you chose. So how did you evade death?"*

"I don't know. Did I?"

*The baby laughs. "Yes, Peter, you did. What is keeping you in
the world? Past, present or future? Which of the scenes we
showed you will you be living in a hundred years?"*

"Why should I be living any?"

*"You will. Unless you die now, you will. It's just a matter of
which one."*

One second had passed since the last beat. His mother was
there. She would cry. No parent should ever see their child

28

die. His mother worried so much about him, and she had been a good mother. Or as good as they come. He couldn't die. Her work would be wasted. If he lived he would remember them. They would live on in him.

Two seconds. He could take this as an opportunity. He could ask out one of the nurses while he was recovering. Pete had heard they had little time to meet people, and were at least flattered by the attention.

Three seconds. The baby was wrong. As was the middle-aged man. His own future? No, he could avoid it. He could achieve what he wanted and then stop. A comfortable life, and no more. Maybe if the others were real he could help them, too. He could stop the killer. Or help the mourner. He had to be able to change things. Where there's life...

Thump.

Four seconds, and the heart began again. Tha-thump. Stronger than before. Tha- thump. The machine's lights flicked back onto normal again. In a Mexican-wave-like effect, sighs of relief ran along the watching group. At the end, near the door, Pete heard the door open. He opened an eye just in time to see a well-dressed balding man, shaking his head and leaving the room.

Innocent Dreaming

Amanda had only just fallen into a fitful sleep - the monsters were no longer crawling along the corridors shooting fireballs at her, and neither were the missiles raining down from the skies towards her three cities. Finally the images behind her eyes had died down, and the sounds of gunfire and explosions were no more.

The quiet voice, then, came as even more of a surprise.

"Amanda..." it began. A very low-pitched, slow voice. Stressing each syllable as if taking an incredible effort. Eventually there was a wheezing noise, like an old man struggling for breath after a coughing fit.

"Mandy," she corrected, out loud. Instinctively she opened her eyes, only to see the ceiling above her, and the globe lampshade hanging in the room's centre. She could not make out the corners of the room, though, and stared towards them in case there was something there. As her heart beat faster, she noticed the throbbing in her temples. A loud thumping which might obliterate any further voices.

That thought did not last long, however. "Mandy," it said again.

"What?" she said, lifting her head slightly in case whatever it was was at the end of the bed. Shambles sometimes came in and sat there, warming herself on Amanda's feet, waiting to be fed.

"I need your help."

"Who are you?" She sat up now - her heart racing so much she knew she would never get back to sleep unless she searched the room. The voice, though, did not sound like it came from outside. It was in her head, but she wanted to search anyway, just to make sure she was imagining it.

"You aren't."

"I'm not what?"

"Imagining it."

Amanda pulled her knees up to her chin and shivered. Her eyes stopped searching around the room and settled on looking directly forwards, wide open. Within moments they began to hurt, but she kept them open anyway.

"What do you want?" she said, louder than before. If her parents had been in, rather than at the Parents' Association dance, she would have tried to scream.

"Stop shivering."

Amanda pulled the duvet up to her chin and edged back towards the headboard. Her hair moved on her back, sending another shiver down her spine.

"Don't be afraid," it wheezed once again, and then everything went silent. Amanda realised there had been a gasping breathing sound, only now obvious because of its absence.

There was a warmth behind her forehead, just in the area she normally imagined headaches living. Something there, a light. As if she could roll her eyes up in her head and see it, glowing there. Then, as fast at it appeared, darkness. Her eyes closed, and she felt distant from her body.

Floating, somewhere, she let her arms swing out, letting them fall into their own place. No light, no sound, no movement. No sensation.

Another light appeared, but she did not open her eyes to see it. A man stood, or maybe floated, in front of her. Are you God? she thought, knowing that he could hear.

"If you like," he replied, his voice no longer gasping for breath, but smooth and precise. He smiled. Despite having no discernible features, he smiled. "A common mistake, and understandable, given your background."

He was not God. Why would God deny Himself? Christ did, of course, or at least never answered directly. She never understood why that was. The nuns didn't want to tell her, and she was afraid of asking again.

"They would not tell you because they are afraid to expose their own foolishness."

Foolishness in what? Believing in God?

"Of course. What else? Any belief beyond your experience."

What are you?

"I need a life, Mandy. I need to live again, and you answered my call."

What call? I didn't do anything!

"You were here, where I needed you, and you were open to me."

Oh Lord, you're the devil aren't you? You've come to possess me oh hail Mary mother of God hail Mary mother of...

"Mandy Mandy Mandy. Show a little dignity, please. I am not the devil. There is no devil. I am simply a man in need of life. Yours."

Why? What have I done?

"Nothing. But I have lost my life, and I need yours to replace it."

But that's not fair!

"No indeed. But then death is not, is it?"

You can't! Oh please God make it stop. Please. I don't want to die. I don't want to.

"Why not?"

Because I don't, all right! I just don't. I've got the disco next week, and my birthday's in a couple of months, and then its Christmas and I'm going to get an upgrade for my computer and a couple of new games and I don't want to mummy make them oh please God...

"Oh well, as long as there is a good reason, that's all right then. Shall I tell you why I want to live?"

No. I don't want...

"Good, then be quiet for a moment. I want to live, dearest Mandy, because I have grown used to it, and because I deserve to. I have fought against much that I believe is wrong, and for much that I believe is right. I have saved more lives than I can count, and I feel I have earned one life in return. And that life is yours."

Why me?

"Because you were here, and you answered."

I didn't!

"You did, Mandy. And if not you, then who else? Whose life would you have me take in your stead? Your mother's, perhaps?"

No. No I don't want you to take anyone's life.

"Calm now, Mandy. Calm. Maybe someone beyond the family? Maybe someone at school? One of the nuns, perhaps? One of the ones that have been lying to you all these years?"

No.

"Then I am afraid, Mandy, that you will die."

Oh please no. Please.

"Then whose life would you have me take?"

I don't know. Just not mine. And not mum's, or dad's or anyone like that. Someone I don't know. Someone old who's going to die anyway.

"I'm afraid I need a healthy life, someone who is still young enough for me. Let me see. Why don't I give you a few minutes to think about it, and make your mind up. If you can't tell me whose life I should take within, say, five minutes, I will have yours."

Amanda hit the floor, groaned and rolled over onto her back, trying desperately to stop quivering. She was on the other side of the room from her bed now. Her Thunderbirds clock said eleven-fifty-five. She had gone to bed at nine-thirty, like she was supposed to.

There was a sudden movement outside the door. The main light switched on. Footsteps, coming towards her door. She panicked and half-crawled, half-ran backwards into the corner of the room.

The door opened, and the light near-blinded her. A tall figure stood in the doorway, his shadow cast across the room. Amanda ran back further into the corner, desperately pushing things between her and him.

"Mandy? It's the middle of the night. What are you doing up?"

It took her another few seconds to work out it was her father's voice, and even then she couldn't stop shaking.

"What's wrong?" he said as he walked over, pushing the toys that lay between them out of the way. "What's happened?"

She allowed him to lift her to her feet, and felt his arms pull her towards him. She shut her eyes again, and felt her shaking subside, slowly ebbing away in the comforting hold of her father.

Eventually he pushed her away and looked down at her. She opened her eyes and squinted back up at him. "I've never seen you so scared. What happened?"

She starting breathing quickly, trying to stop herself from bursting into tears. "It was a bad dream," she said, still trying to convince herself. "A really really bad dream. I thought someone was going to kill me."

Her father breathed a sigh of relief. "Then it's over. Are you going to be all right, or do you want me to stay in here for a while to check you're all right."

He used to do that when she was scared. He would say that he was going to stay until the morning to check that the monsters under her bed didn't crawl up and bite her toes off. She used to laugh, and slept soundly. Until her thirteenth birthday, when she woke up in the middle of the night and saw that he had gone. He never offered any more.

"No, daddy. I'll be fine. It was just a dream."

He nodded slowly, in exactly the way she expected.

She went back to bed, and he tucked her in and sat on the edge of the bed, looking down at her, the worried frown still on his face. He leant down and kissed her on the forehead, the way he had always done when she was little, and said good-night. Then he stood up and walked out, pulling the door to behind him. Just as he was leaving she fought back a sudden urge to shout after him: "No, please. Stay tonight. Please stay."

She looked over at her clock. Eleven-fifty-nine. The red lights in the middle flashed twice while she was watching.

She rolled onto her back, stretched her legs out and shut her eyes.

Almost as if she'd opened a door, the man was waiting for her.

"Well?"

She tried to scream, but nothing happened.

She pulled her legs up, pushing them against the bedclothes, trying to move away. The bed seemed to move, but she remained. The man was just as close.

She rolled over, reaching for the head-board to pull herself away. It was already beyond reach. The bed seemed larger now, and the man was on top of it, almost on top of her.

She pulled herself up onto her knees and began crawling towards the edge of the bed, but it kept the same distance away. Behind her the bed seemed to grow and grow, and she became smaller and smaller.

He reached down and picked her up by the scruff of the neck. She felt a warm trickle down her leg.

"Well?" he repeated.

She struggled, but her punches and kicks didn't even reach. She shut her eyes, clenching them shut, wanting to wake up, or be somewhere else.

"Please," she began, whimpering, not believing for a moment that he would release her.

"Who then?" he asked, quiet as anything.

She kicked and grabbed at his hand, pulling herself up so she could bite it. The bed was long gone now, and as she looked down she saw endless black below. And above. And all around. She shivered, and began pulling desperately at the man's fingers, trying to prize them off her.

"Who?" he asked, slightly louder.

"No!" she screamed, her legs flailing as she tried to pull a single finger off her. He was holding her neck now, and both of her hands together hardly fitted round one of his fingers. She gave in to the tears.

"Who?"

As her mind realised there was no point struggling, her body tensed - all the muscles straining to do something, however insignificant. Her heart raced, and she could hardly talk.

"WHO?" The sound nearly deafened her.

She hung, suddenly limp again, surrendering. "Not me," she whimpered.

"WHO THEN?"

"Anyone. Please, not me."

"Your father," he ventured, quiet again.

"Yes," she said, shaking her head in despair. "Anyone."

The grip on her neck stopped, and all about her was dark. She fell, tumbling through the darkness, feeling herself accelerating, but still unable to see anything. She felt dizzy.

She landed on her right hip, hitting it into the corner of the bed. She screamed, but this time the noise rang round the room.

Her mother came this time, and found her lying on her side at the edge of the bed, unable to move.

"What's happened now?" asked her mother, rushing over. "Oh Amanda! Surely you should be able to stop yourself falling out of bed at your age!"

Her mother lifted her up and helped her onto the bed.

"Is daddy all right?" Amanda asked, clutching at her mother's shoulders.

"He's asleep, as you should be. It's one o'clock!"

"Please could you check?"

"Why?"

"Please? I just had this really awful dream, and I..." She realised how stupid it sounded, but it didn't stop her wanting to know.

"Are you going to be able to sleep, or should I get you something to help you?"

"I'll be okay," Amanda replied, sliding back underneath the duvet.

Her mother walked out of the room, and Amanda knew she would not sleep a wink that night, not until she knew one way or the other. Whether she had killed her own father or not.

The morning light came as welcome relief from her staring towards the ceiling. She ran downstairs the moment it reached seven o'clock.

She filled the kettle, poured a small jug of milk, fetched the milk bottles in from the porch, and generally busied herself for as long as possible. But her parents had still not yet risen.

At last, after preparing the whole breakfast, she sat down at the table and waited. It seemed to take her parents longer than usual to rise, but then usually she was hoping they would sleep in.

When at last she heard her father stirring, she ran upstairs. He was still in his dressing-gown, on the way to the shower. She stopped him, grabbing him by the arm and turning him. He looked down at her, surprised into silence.

"Daddy," she began.

"Yes?"

"Are you all right?" She looked down at the floor, her cheeks blushing with embarrassment. Are you all right? Have you been possessed overnight?

"I'm fine. Why? What's going on?"

Did he sound normal? Was this the same man who had tucked her in last night?

She turned and walked off downstairs again, ignoring the comments her parents made behind her. Overnight things had changed, and her father would never be the same again, because she would never know for sure.

Inspiration

An image floated towards him through the mists, slowly taking shape. As he recognised it, the ever-present ringing in his ears abated slightly, allowing him to hear the words. "Come on George, aren't you ready yet? We're going shopping."

Sixty people die of natural causes one by one and you wouldn't bat an eyelid, right?

Sixty people just lay down and die in a shopping centre, all at the same time, and you start wondering (a) what's going on, (b) why you do such a stupid job, and (c) what you've been drinking.

Jerry used to say I shouldn't joke, and Harv said my attitude was childish and immature. Given the circumstances, though, I thought it was the only way to survive.

It's not even like it was a place I didn't know - I take Maggie and the kids out there every Wednesday night to go shopping. Usually we wander up to the computer games shop up on the second floor, and I let Kev choose something he wants. I think Maggie takes Julie down to the toy shop at the same time, and she gets something, too. Back at University I would have said that style of parenting was appalling, but hell - you get into the real world and you just go along with it all. It doesn't make sense, but it's easy.

When I got there Tuesday night I went up to the computer shop first, like I was expecting to find someone I knew. In the end, fortunately, none of Kev's classmates were in there. There was a total of eight children dead. I took them back, same as always, and I can't find shit wrong with them. It's just like they laid down and gave up living.

By Wednesday it was all cleaned up and everything was open again, but we didn't go. We went to the superstore up near the station. Kev screamed and sulked all night at not getting a new game. I said he was spoilt anyway, and left Maggie with the problem. I had work to do.

Sixty dead, and not one cause of death between them.

Even old age usually has something. You know, they die of "old age" but really die of a cold or something. Sure there were the smokers, the drinkers, the fat and lazy office workers, and all combinations of the above, but none of them should have been dead. So, in my naïveté, I wrote that into my report.

Harv dragged me up to his office and shouted at me for twenty minutes. I didn't try to argue - the press was on his back, and he wasn't used to that kind of publicity. Hell, this is a quiet town, and I don't think there's anywhere in the world that would find this sort of thing routine.

On the way home I switched on the radio. After skipping through the news reports on five stations, I found one playing music. "These things you say... they're unbelievable." I couldn't help laughing.

George looked down from the top level of the shopping centre, down towards the people on the escalators below. They all looked the same - hazy blobs moving about on a landscape he knew rather than saw. As he looked down on the tiny homogenous figures, he noticed that all the escalators pointed towards the games shop. His mum was three floors down, just starting to get worried about him. George couldn't make her out, that far down, but he knew she would be worrying.

He took the lift down and walked into the shop. Demonstrations of all the recent games he couldn't afford to buy, and didn't have a powerful enough computer to play anyway. It seemed so stupid the way they kept making them more and more expensive. Or was the stupid thing that people kept buying them?

He walked out again, and only then noticed the tinkling of electronic notes flying around. Without warning, the ringing sound in his ears disappeared, allowing the strange notes to flow into his head unhindered.

He ran, instinctively scratching at his forehead, trying to get to the toilets to escape.

To his horror the muzak was still playing inside. Before he could decide what to do, the music was inside him. He left the toilets, looking for his mum. She would know what to do. She always did.

As the tinnitus came back, the sound continued flowing round his head, pushing out into his skull. It was calming music, designed to make shopping more pleasant. George looked over towards the games shop. He felt his face turning red, then blue in the effort to make the sounds go away. Trying to put his fortress of ringing back to normal. He imagined rolling his eyes back and forcing the calm feelings out.

This time it worked. The sounds went away, and the ringing was all that was left, with some background noise penetrating from beyond.

When he opened his eyes he saw his mother in front of him. She looked at him for a second, then fell to the ground.

It's stupid, but it's the way places like that work. Something big happens, and someone has to make sort it out. If it doesn't get sorted out, they sack someone. In this case, me.

So there I was, out of a job, still puzzling over the whole thing. The worst thing was, unlike any of the other deaths I've dealt with, there wasn't an explanation. Usually we get blanks and we don't know enough, but there are usually lots of options. Here we just didn't have a clue.

I got a job over at the University four weeks later. Maggie stopped having her series of breakdowns about money, and went back to complaints about the kids and how I never saw her any more. I spent four weeks at home and she didn't like that either. No pleasing some people.

No one in their right mind could complain about the standard of my work, so I fitted in quickly and carved myself a little niche. Four courses and eight Ph.D. students, along with my own work. Quite a hectic schedule, but I enjoyed the work so I could spend the time. It's the great thing about Uni. over anywhere else - the people who bother to turn up are genuinely interested in knowing what you've got to say. Maybe it's just to pass, sure, but at least you've got their attention. There are a few I think I really got through to.

Anyway, this continued for seven months or so before the 'accident'. I'm not sure I should call it an accident, because strictly speaking it wasn't, but any incident involving cars crashing always gets described as an accident, and I don't have a better word for it.

It was summer, and hot at that, so we had the windows wound down. We were just on the way home, coming up to the junction where we turn right to get to our house. The lights were just turning red, and this black Ford Capri raced past, music blaring.

Obviously it expected the car in front to keep going, so it slammed on its brakes and honked its horn a couple of times. All the cars are still moving at this point, you understand.

The lights go red, and the car in front of the Capri suddenly accelerated away. The Capri raced after it.

Now to this day I can't remember what happened - not really - but I know that I accelerated across too. I certainly don't know why. All the cars behind me, as well. The traffic going the other way couldn't get onto the junction, and the cars were still coming by the time the lights turned back to green again.

According to police cameras, the cars continued coming through for almost four minutes, with a train of cars nearly half a mile long racing down this road.

Then we all come to the next junction. Again I went straight on for some reason, and neither Maggie nor the kids complained at me. Or at least they don't remember doing so, and I don't remember anything.

The next junction was red, which was where the trouble started. The other traffic was already going across, and the front car - the one that accelerated away first, got smashed sideways by a lorry going across. The Capri and the car next to it carry on through regardless, and the other traffic there is forced to stop, too.

By the time we reach the motorway half an hour later, the police had become aware of us all. Also, the convoy had fallen to about half its original size, partly due to cars running out of petrol. We were still going along, two columns, about eighty miles an hour, not stopping for anything. Before we reached the motorway there were eighteen collisions and two people are dead, including the driver of that first car.

The police, only for the second time in history, closed off the motorway and set up a roadblock. Turned out that was about the worst thing they could do.

I begin to remember better at this point, just as the roadblock comes into view. There was music blasting out from the Capri - loud rock music. I could hear it in our car, even though we were three cars back in the convoy.

The Capri was still at the head, with another Ford next to it - a Sierra I think. There were two adults in it, but I can't really remember what they look like. The only occupant I can remember was the child - a boy of about fifteen. He was moving about, shaking to the sound of the music, almost bashing himself into the sides of the car. His eyes were closed, and he kept turning his head back and forth.

The front two cars slammed straight into the roadblock. The Capri driver was killed instantly, as were the two adults in the other front car. Forty-six people died in the collisions, including Kev. Turned out his car seat was the wrong sort and he was strangled by it. The airbags saved me and Maggie, and Julie's seat was the right type, although she was in hospital for two weeks from minor injuries - the hospital said minor, I thought they looked serious.

In questioning, only four of the survivors remembered anything about what had happened, but all of them remembered the boy. The odd thing was, though, that the firemen on the scene couldn't find any trace of him. They said that if there had been a boy there he'd have been killed, especially if he was moving about like we described, as it suggested no seatbelt.

It made top slot of national news for two weeks running, that story, as I'm sure you remember. No one could explain it. Fortunately no one even tried to suggest some sort of suicide conspiracy. If they'd suggested we intended it I think it would have been even harder to get our heads around.

Maggie started going to a survivors' group. I went to the first one, but I prefer to keep my feelings to myself most of the time, so I didn't bother again. I think it hit Julie hardest of all. Maggie and I had always thought she hated Kev, but she broke down completely. That was good in a way, though - Maggie kept herself together to help Julie out, and the two of them became much closer. I wouldn't say they're over it even now, but they're getting there.

The seemingly-endless hum of the engine began to pierce the ringing. He knew what was coming - he had felt it before. As the ringing died down, the clarity of the world's noise was almost painful. He lowered his head, hoping that placing his hands over his ears would stop the pain this time.

George felt the wind rushing into his ears, screaming of the places it had been - of its freedom. He clenched his fists, trying to blot out the sounds, to make them go away again.

The engine sound became quieter. He hoped it was the ringing returning, but it was not. The car was slowing down. Another engine sound in front. And behind. And on the left.

He screwed his eyes shut, pushing fingers into his ears. He began to moan slightly, and heard his foster-mother ask him if he was okay. He felt breathless, though, and couldn't answer. Shut the window! he thought, but said nothing. Just kept moaning.

"George?" he heard, loud and piercing, far too loud.

Another engine, and something else. A loud beating sound. Words. Loud, passionate words. Really loud. Blotting out everything around.

One sound was less painful than the cacophony, so he concentrated on it, tried to home in on it, listening to every beat, every word, every scream of the instruments.

He kept his eyes shut, but they were no longer screwed tight. He relaxed and allowed the music to wash over him. His head began to move to the rhythm of the music, to its loud ever-present beat.

The cars accelerated forwards, its speed increasing as the music built to a frenzy. There were other sounds, now - horns and screams. Screeching. They came in time, building on the music. Everything built on it, making it more and more, pushing it to the limits. Even the movement of the car, the engine sound, it became part of the song.

Now most people probably live through something they can't explain - you know, like seeing a UFO or something. But two occasions when people spontaneously do something unnatural - I couldn't help wondering if they were linked. And I couldn't help wondering if that boy was the key to the whole thing.

I have to admit I thought any link between the two was unlikely, but no one had anything to go on regarding the car madness, so I thought I might as well. Things were getting worse at home, and I hadn't spoken to Maggie for days, so I was desperate to get out of the house, too. Kev's death seemed to have brought her and Julie closer, but at the expense of shutting me out. I knew I was losing her, but I honestly didn't know what I could do about it.

The police had had interviews with all the people in the shopping centre that day, and I had a copy still kicking about. I'd copied everything about that case before they got rid of me.

It took me two hours to find it all, but when I did, the link leapt out at me. A boy, thirteen years old, profoundly deaf and partially sighted, had lost his mother. Father unknown. There was a photo of him, too, and although he'd obviously changed, I still recognised him. George Cates was his name. The report said he was going into care. Presumably they'd have found a foster home as quickly as possible, so he would have gone to another family - might even have changed his name. I don't know the procedure for that sort of thing.

Anyway, he didn't have a foster family any more, as the accident claimed both of them, so I wondered what had happened to him. Since I still know a few people in high places, I started to inquire.

Turned out he inherited the quite sizeable fortune that his foster-parents had - held in trust of course until he was of age. He also got moved again. I got the address, and went round there.

As I arrived I saw George leaving. He was cycling furiously down the road, so I turned the car round and followed him.

He went back to his old family's house. An enormous detached place, sitting in a protecting square of pine trees. When he got to the front door he took ages to unlock it, and left it ajar behind him. Careless, but he was only a kid.

I left the car on the street and walked in after him. As soon as I pushed the door open I could hear sounds, distant notes echoing around the house. And a slight thumping.

I walked up the stairs and along a hallway. The noise became louder as I reached a large wooden door on the right. Apart from that door, I don't remember anything about the place. Only really that the huge black door was so different that it didn't fit it at all, like I was about to enter another world. I remember thinking that.

I listened at it for a few moments, and realised that the music behind the door was Beethoven. After waiting for a few seconds more, I pushed the door open. The blast of volume almost knocked me back.

I covered my ears, but it was still deafening. I think I fell back onto the carpet at that point, allowing the door to swing open.

Inside there was this huge room, empty of everything except a CD player on the opposite side of the room and two enormous speakers. George was standing in the centre of the room, his arms stretched wide, as if reaching for something. He was facing away from me.

As the music grew louder, a blue glow appeared on his fingertips. Suddenly, on a beat of the music, it shot into the ceiling - a single strand from each finger. George pushed his fingers down and flew upwards into the centre of the room. Just like that.

The music continued to rise, louder and louder. I think I felt the pain in my ears, or at least I was aware of it, but I don't know - the scene unfolding in front of me made the pain not just bearable but almost insignificant.

Lights began to flicker in front of George. Flying and swirling. I sat entranced, drawn into the flickering images. For a moment I saw a boy, running, racing through a forest. Then moonlight. A lake, reflecting the moon, and freedom. I saw freedom.

The room had become invisible to me, and there was nothing but the music. Nothing but the experience, the whole. Then I was lost in the feeling - the joy of freedom.

George knew this room as home.

Wherever it was, in whatever house, this room was home.

The only possessions he valued, the CD player and the CDs

themselves. Ever since his mother's death, these were the only things that kept him going. Kept him suffering different families, different people, and all the moving about.

He pretended to them all, of course, that he was happy and contended. Any reluctance to talk they put down to his disabilities.

Here, though, he could do the one thing in the world he enjoyed. He could play music loudly enough that he could hear it, ringing or no ringing. Loudly enough that he could feel it. Once inside, it began coursing through his veins, playing as loudly from within as without.

Today he put on Beethoven's Ode to Joy. He checked that the volume knob was set to full, and stepped back into the middle of the room. He pressed the play button on the remote, and then tossed it into the corner of the room.

As the first notes sounded in his ears, the feeling and the power rushed through him. He threw his arms up, loving it, breathing it. His fingers tensed, tendons pulling with all their might, trying to hold in the passion.

And then, when there was almost pain, a release. The feeling went from him, and he was floating, totally engrossed in the music. No longer from the speakers, but from inside or from all around - he couldn't tell.

When he awoke, he still felt echoes of the music, a warm feeling. The memory of happiness. But it was never enough. It was always slightly bitter, knowing that he never remembered the time itself, the full flights of passion he knew were in the music.

The next thing I remember is George waking me up. He brought me a glass of water, and apologised to me - I don't know what for.

I felt very weak for a while, but George stayed with me. I spent the time asking him about the accident, and the strange occurrence at the shopping centre, and what I had just seen. I made an effort to commit his accounts to memory, and I found the process of piecing together this strange boy's life deeply affecting, as if he had been born in the wrong time to the wrong people. I don't know where that feeling came from, but it was there.

When I recovered and we had finished talking, he asked me what I was going to do. I replied that I had to tell a colleague, just so they knew what was going on.

George went and sat on a chair in the corner of the dining room, as if I were a teacher and had told him off. I went to the phone and rang Jerry, my ex-colleague from back at the lab. I gibbered at him for a couple of minutes, and he agreed to come over - I suspected he was more worried about my mental health than anything else.

He seemed to take forever to arrive - I was waiting at the door. Before he had even got inside, I began telling him the story. He looked at me as if I was mad.

"But I can prove it..." I began.

He shook his head. "You're trying to pin all these deaths on the boy, just so you can understand it. That's wrong, John."

"But I can prove it to you. He told me what happened - he was the cause of both tragedies. I can show you."

I led him through to the dining room, but George had disappeared. I heard a door slam upstairs, and some music started. A quiet, rhythmic beating. Almost like a train running over the breaks between rails. Repeating, over and over again. Bum badadabum badadabum...

I looked up towards the room, and then rushed out into the hall.

"Come on," I shouted at Jerry.

He ran up the stairs behind me. By the time we got to the door, I recognised the music: Ravel's Bolero. I pushed open the door.

Sure enough, George was floating in the middle, flying round the room, his circles getting smaller and higher, moving towards the centre of the ceiling.

I heard Jerry draw breath and then suddenly become stock-still, staring into the scene, lost in it. When I looked at George's face it was a picture of tragedy, of pain. He cried as he circled the room, occasional whimpers mixing in with the music, building on it.

They died out as the music grew, and I realised where it was going. I screamed for him to stop, but that too seemed in time with the music, fitting in with the building power. I ran forwards and hit the stop button on the CD player, but it continued. Even louder. And George was nearly at the top of the room.

I ran for the plug and pulled it out, knowing it wouldn't make a difference, but it was in time with the music too, somehow. It was what I had to do. From near the speakers it was obvious now - the music was not coming from them.

George was spinning so quickly I became dizzy watching him, screaming at him to stop. At the top of the room he paused for a second and looked down. The gap before the final bar of music seemed to take forever.

He mouthed "sorry" at me.

I tried to scream at him, to tell him it wasn't his fault, that there was a difference between cause and responsibility, but my cry took too long.

Before I made a sound he fell to the floor like a shot bird.

I turned and looked away, unable to go to the body.

Jerry had fallen into unconsciousness. He fell into a coma, where he's been ever since.

I called an ambulance. They came, and immediately called the police. The first thing they did was arrest me and charge me with the murder.

That's it, really. That's what happened. I don't care if you believe me or not - that's up to you. I'm going to be found guilty, but I don't care. I don't think I could ever care about anything much anymore - not after feeling that music. All I want to do is remember as much as I can for as long as I can. Forgetting that feeling will be more painful than any imprisonment could ever be.

King Arthur, Samantha, and Batman

"Hi, Bruce Wayne," said Dave, looking at the photo he'd picked up from the last works do. He shook his head, depressed again.

They loved him at work - they said so. He cheered them all up, and stopped them taking things too seriously. Even one of the managers had once admitted that he was good for morale.

Everyone apart from Sam, anyway. She didn't even know him. They had shared eighteen words over the time Dave had been working there - almost two years now. And out of all the people in the office, she was the only one he wanted to talk to.

Merlin walked up behind him. "My lord," he began.

Dave turned. "Merlin, what are you doing here?"

"My lord, I have come to warn you."

Arthur smiled. "You always bring warnings, Merlin. When will you bring me good news? The kingdom flourishes, as it has for years. Camelot is complete. My knights are well respected and well loved. What is there to warn about?"

Merlin looked down at Guinevere's portrait. Arthur was still holding it close to him - the only image of her he possessed. Merlin, he felt sure, could conjure something closer to the real thing. "Your love for the lady," he began. "It will undo your greatest works. It will ruin the kingdom."

"How so?" asked the king, and then remembered. Lancelot.

Why did he always pick such tragic stories to play out? Why stories where good things didn't happen? Dave shook his head.

"No, Merlin," said the king. "It could be different this time."

"No, sire. It will always be as it has always been. She will desert you, and you will tear the kingdom apart in your rage. Think of what you have achieved."

The king shook his head, sure there was something missing from Merlin's analysis. He stood up, letting the photo fall to the floor. The oven was on, and he hadn't put the lasagne in yet. If he didn't eat soon, he'd be up late again, and then he'd not sleep well and he'd feel exhausted all the next day. Every time Dave thought like that he felt very old.

The lasagne safely popped into the oven, Dave walked upstairs and lay down on the bed. He stared up at the ceiling. The sun was just setting, and the curtain rail - or rather the curtain wire that he still hadn't got round to fixing - made a long shadow across the ceiling.

"Hi, Bruce Wayne," he said, again.

"Sam," came the reply. A posh party, like the one Vicky Vale had been seduced at. Came down to the money, then?

Suddenly it was dark. The batcave. Computers all around him. The schoolboy's fantasy. Dave wondered if schoolboys still fantasised about computers, now that they lived with them every day of the week.

Bruce pushed a couple of buttons, and the lights behind him came on. The car rose up out of the ground and turned round. That turntable had always been a part of this kind of fantasy -

right from the toy cars and the train set he'd had as a child.

Vicky walked down the stairs. "Bruce," she began.

"No," he replied, his voice suddenly deeper. "Not tonight."

She was right next to him. He had hardly noticed her move. Her green eyes stared right into his. "Who are you?"

"I'm Batman." He smiled, remembering how difficult Michael Keaton had found saying those words.

"I love you."

Stupid words. I lust after you, perhaps. They always did. But understand? Never. Bruce understood, he knew what he needed, and he knew what he wanted. Two very separate things. You prowl the night, the girl you need doesn't come looking. The wrong sort does, of course.

"I've got to go to work."

Running away again. He stood up. The cloak billowed behind as he ran to the car. Somehow the run never involved his feet touching the floor - that would remove the perfection. The cloak billowed and he was there. Like the bat. By the time he returned, she was gone.

Again, he thought. Another tragedy. "Why is that, Alfred?"

"Sir?" he replied, in his usual unworried tone.

"She left me."

"You drove her away, sir."

At work he sat at his desk, tapping away cross-legged on the chair - that really irritated his boss, but it was more comfortable. Every ten minutes or so he stopped and spun round on the chair, taking a look at the office as they looked at him.

"Why am I always separate?" he mumbled to himself.

"Because you are king," replied Merlin, serious as ever. "You must remain aloof, so the people can idolise you."

"But is that not wrong? Should I not be their leader rather than their god?"

"They are interchangeable," said Merlin, and promptly disappeared.

Dave thought about it for a while, and then settled back into his typing. Separateness. So he didn't like the world very much? That wasn't a crime. It shouldn't stand against him, just because he didn't take it seriously.

Except he did, he just tried not to.

He hid behind the mask. The bat. Or the sword.

"Dave?" Rich was next to him, sitting there already. No warning. Dave hated sitting with his back to the main part of the office.

"Yeah?" said Dave, picking up a paper fish he'd made the previous day and prodding Rich with it.

"We're going for a drink on Friday. Fancy coming along?" Rich smiled. A normal, friendly smile. He was a normal, friendly person. Down to earth, not screwed up, chatted to people when he felt like it.

"What do you think, Mr Fish?" he asked of the fish. He waved it next to his ear for a moment. "Mr Fish doesn't like drinking. He says he won't drink anything his friends have fornicated in."

"You're mad," said Rich. All Dave's friends said that, sooner or later. "So do you want to?"

"Why not?" said Dave. Why not a yes? Why couldn't he be enthusiastic? Probably because he didn't know whether he'd feel enthusiastic enough to spend the night having fun playing or whether something would bring him back into the real world. Something or someone. Like Sam.

"Good. We might as well pick up a chinese and head back to my place, so we can go straight from work."

With that Rich was off, back to his dull routine. Rich disliked his job, but never got round to doing anything about it. Dave could never understand that.

Friday came.

"My lord," began Merlin.

"Merlin," said the king. "I am busy."

"I wished to warn you away from this evening's entertainments. The feast. I believe it would be a mistake."

Arthur turned round to face Merlin. Merlin was standing, staring off into space. "Why?" asked the king.

"Your lady is of another world, my lord. If you leave here,

your works will be undone."

The king understood. He couldn't leave. This was his life. His kingdom had to mean more than his own emotions. It was selfish to believe otherwise. "Thank you, Merlin," he said, dismissing his faithful adviser as firmly as he ever had.

"Alfred?"

The old man appeared. The sky disappeared, replaced with dark rock. "Sir?"

"What do you think?"

"You came down here for a reason, sir. Without it you will be half of what you are now. But it is your judgement that matters, sir."

The background disappeared again, replaced by a ledge of rock, just in time for Bruce to collapse to his knees and scream, clawing at the ground. "To leave or not to leave," he began, and then thought better of effecting another shift.

At lunchtime, a good morning's work completed - mainly to take his mind off that evening - Dave went for a walk down by the canal. As soon as he arrived, of course, it changed. A lake stretched out in front of him.

"My lady," he whispered as he sat down.

"My lord," came the eerie voice from the water.

"I have not asked your opinion on the matter."

There was a slight movement under the water, but no one appeared. A barge floated past, slowly. Dave waited until it had gone to continue his conversation.

"My king, what are you afraid of?"

"She will turn me down."

"You have not lost anything, and you have been turned down before," came the voice, now internal. "Your majesty can survive that."

"It would be doomed anyway. I could not live like her - going to clubs and drinking and chatting all the time. And I am needed here. Merlin is warning of the death of the kingdom again."

The lady thought for some time before replying. "Merlin is right. The kingdom is dying..."

"Why? What can be done?"

"...just as you are dying. Someday it will end. But that is not important. Your rule will have given us a few decades of prosperity, and no one can ever destroy that, no matter what becomes of the kingdom."

"But I can build something that will last. Something that will live forever."

"No, my lord. You cannot. You can build during your life. When you reach the end, or when the kingdom falls, you can stand back and bask in the glories you have achieved. After that, it is the job of another."

"So is all this really for naught? Are the struggles to build the perfect kingdom futile?"

"If you think of them like that, yes. They are."

"How else can I think of them?"

"A bright light, shining for a short time in a long night. The light is good, but the candle will burn out."

"And Guinevere?"

"The same. If she is with you for a year, is that not enough? Would you rather you had a year than nothing?"

"Why not forever?"

"Because forever, my lord, is never." Abruptly, she was silent.

Dave waited a moment for anything further, and then stood up. "Thank you, lady. As ever, you are wise." He bowed towards the canal, and then turned and walked back into the office.

The night itself.

Dave sat nervously waiting. He didn't know if his courage would last, and prayed he would get the chance this time. It was now or never. He knew that. But how many times had he said that before, only to repeat it again the next week?

She walked into the bar. Beautiful as ever. He heard Rich's sharp intake of breath as he watched her find a table and sit down. Her friend - female - went to the bar to order drinks.

Rich turned to Dave, as if prompting. Dave took a deep breath. He shut his eyes and counted to five. Just to steady his nerves a little. He knew, though, this time. At the end of five. Rich began to say something, but stopped as Dave opened his eyes and stood up.

Dave began the walk over to her table, but Arthur ended it. He leant slightly over the table. "My lady," he said. "May I?"

"Sure," she said, looking slightly puzzled. He had to admit he liked that look.

"Merlin warned me against talking to you," he began, in a slightly hushed tone. "But I had to anyway. I trust I am not intruding?" She shook her head. "He believes you will be the death of the kingdom, while the lady of the lake believes you would be a light for the people to delight in."

Her friend arrived at the table. Arthur stood up.

"This is Jo," said Sam. "Sorry, I don't know your name..."

"Arthur. King Arthur Pendragon. I am honoured to make your acquaintance, my lady," he said, bowing low.

Jo blushed. Sam smiled. A beautiful smile. Almost worth losing a kingdom for. Almost.

Dave shook his head. "I do apologise. He gets everywhere. One minute you're sitting having a quiet drink, and the next there you are - King Arthur. Terribly embarrassing. Especially in this day and age." He turned to Jo. "Obviously I'm not King Arthur." Then back to Sam again. "Hi," he said. "Bruce Wayne."

He held out a hand, smiling as confidently as he could. His heart was pounding. Enter my world, please enter my world. Only for a while, maybe, but enter my world.

She looked down at the hand. Then, slowly at first, her hand moved to hold it. "Mr Wayne," she replied. His heart leapt. The door flew open, and a light shone through it. A king stood on the other side, welcoming his queen. A hero, welcoming a fellow traveller, someone to trust. Visitors in the realms.

"Call me Bruce," he said.

"All right. Bruce. How are you?"

"To be honest," he replied. "It's complicated. You know how some people have a sort of double life...?"

Leonardo From Two Angles

"The most exciting find in a decade", they had said. "You should be proud." But Harvey wasn't proud. He was terrified. They'd kill him when he told them. When he'd found out, he'd gone straight home to Louise.

Although she'd given him a key two months before, he still rang the doorbell. She opened it, and despite having a headache from staring at one of the Magic Eye books for the past hour, took one look at how pale Harvey was and helped him to a chair. She boiled a kettle and brought him a mug of tea before asking what was wrong.

"It's a forgery," he said, and then turned to her. She sat on the edge of the chair and put an arm round, feeling him trembling with fear.

"But I thought they'd done tests...?" she began, unsure quite how such tests were done, but certain Harvey had mentioned something about it when he'd first got the project.

He took a couple of deep breaths and a sip of the tea before he tried to speak again. Louise ran a hand up and down his shoulder as he waited.

"They had, but only on small sections. Those sections date from the end of the fifteenth century, which is correct. Unfortunately today I began the restoration work on the bottom-right corner, where the signature is."

"And?" she asked, unsure if Harvey was going to tell her without further prompting.

"And it came off."

Louise's eyes opened wide and she gulped. "Oh, dear," she said. Her boyfriend had defaced a previously-unknown work by Leonardo da Vinci. She didn't quite know the etiquette for such situations.

"Precisely. I didn't panic, though, because I was working really carefully and only one flake came off before I began wondering why. The solution we use is supposed to leave the oils intact. So I took the flake down to the lab and had it analysed again. Turns out it was added a century later."

"So who really did the painting?"

"The brushwork is da Vinci, the style is his, everything says he did it. Apart from the signature."

"So maybe he just didn't sign it."

Harvey shook his head. "No. It's finished. He'd have signed it. Which means one of his contemporaries copied him and wanted to leave the ambiguity."

"Why wouldn't they have forged his signature?"

"I don't know. Maybe they felt guilty about it and decided to abandon the painting after completion. I don't know. I just know that it's not the painting we were led to believe it was."

Harvey took another sip of tea and then hugged Louise for a good ten minutes. She kept her eyes shut, trying to throw off her headache rather than try to think of a way to help Harvey.

He would know what to do, and if he didn't she sure as heck wouldn't be able to think of something he hadn't thought of. He was good at his job, and he lived for it. It mattered more to him than anything. Possibly even her.

The next day Harvey went back in to the museum, wondering whether he should tender his resignation, whether he should go to his boss immediately, or whether he should try to find out more about the painting before he said anything.

He chose the latter course, partly because it meant he didn't have to talk to anyone just yet. Harvey liked his boss - Mr Jones was an easily-liked man who invited Harvey and Louise round for dinner at least once a month - but he didn't feel like laying the news of a forgery on him just yet.

Opening the door to the workshop, Harvey instinctively flicked the light-switch, even though the lights were already on. The room went dark, someone shouted at him, and he flicked them back on again. The bulbs took a couple of seconds to flicker into life, and he saw that Mr Jones and two other men were standing looking down at the painting, one of them with a magnifying glass.

"Morning Mr Jones," said Harvey. Mr Jones turned and smiled, but said nothing.

"Harvey McGann?" asked the taller of the two men, both of whom were wearing blue suits. Harvey hated blue suits - he didn't know why.

"Yes."

"We understand from Mr Jones that you have been restoring this painting?" The shorter of the two men, a man with a rather blotchy face, had moved around to the bottom-right corner of the painting, and was looking at it closely. Harvey sighed.

"Yes."

"Then if you would care to explain to us why the end of the signature has been removed?" asked the blotchy-faced man. The tall man turned to him, as if questioning his authority to speak.

Mr Jones interjected: "Mr Falworth and Mr Ingrams are from the board of the museum trust, Harvey. They heard about the analysis you had the lab do yesterday."

Harvey shut his eyes for a moment, wondering if lying was an alternative. He decided it wasn't. "I had begun the restoration work, and I discovered that the signature has been added since the painting was made - a century later, in fact."

"How can that be?" asked Mr Jones. "The brushwork is perfect. It has to be genuine."

"I agree," said Harvey. "But that doesn't change the fact that the signature itself is not. Therefore the restoration work should remove it."

"But if this gets out..." began the tall man.

"It should make no difference," said Mr Jones.

"Of course it *shouldn't*," said the blotchy-faced man, "but it still will. And the museum will not raise the money from it if it isn't genuine. Even a shadow of a doubt would be enough to reduce its value to almost nothing."

The tall man turned to Mr Jones. "Is this man the best restorer you have?" he asked, waving a hand towards Harvey.

"He is."

"Then carry on, I suppose. But leave the signature, so we could return it to the state it was in before you touched it. We've invested a lot in this painting already, you know."

Harvey nodded. The two men walked past him, leaving him alone with Mr Jones.

Mr Jones began saying something, but decided against it and walked past Harvey and out of the room, closing the door behind him. Harvey sat down on a stool next to the painting and stared down at it.

As he stared at it, the whole bottom-right section attracted his attention. An area of almost-uniform black. If didn't seem to quite fit in with the textured areas around it, and Harvey found himself leaning over the painting, trying to work out what it was about the area that was bothering him.

He took another flake of paint from near the signature, and had that analysed. The report, along with the two directors of the trust, returned that afternoon.

"What is the meaning of this?" asked the blotchy-faced man as he slammed the lab results down on the bench.

"I don't know," said Harvey. He tried to think of an explanation. "I think someone did some sort of restoration job on this painting sometime in the sixteenth century. If we remove the added paint, we will probably find another signature underneath."

"Why would anyone cover the signature? It doesn't make sense."

"Perhaps to hide the painting from someone? I don't know. As far as I can see, that is the only altered section."

The two men walked away a little and spoke quietly to each other for a couple of minutes, just loudly enough that Harvey could make out his own name a couple of times, and just quietly enough that he couldn't hear what they were saying about him.

"How confident are you that you could put the signature back if you removed it completely?" the taller man asked.

Harvey looked down at the painting. Either it was a forgery or it wasn't. Either way it was an impressive work of art, and it shouldn't matter which it was. Without the additions it still dated from the fifteenth century. Whatever happened he wanted to see it properly restored to its full glory and placed on display. No matter what it took.

"Sir, if you give me the go-ahead to fully restore it, I give you my personal guarantee there is a signature underneath that area of paint. It is definitely a da Vinci, and therefore it has to be signed. It's as simple as that." Harvey held his hands behind his back, hoping they wouldn't want to shake hands - his were almost dripping with sweat.

"We'll bring this up at the board meeting on Thursday. Don't touch it 'til then."

"All right."

Harvey took the next two days off, waiting for word. Louise skipped her lectures, and they spent the time together, catching up with the gossip from the last couple of weeks that Harvey had missed due to being at work for such long hours.

As they finished the second bottle of wine that afternoon, he began wondering how he had been so lucky as to find Louise. She had been his student the year before, until he had been made the offer by the museum. There had been some bad blood at the University when he'd told them he was moving, but there was little they could do. In a way it was flattering that they would miss him so much, but in another way terrifying that he couldn't go back.

At the board meeting on Thursday, they gave Harvey the go-ahead to restore fully. He went in that afternoon, much to Louise's disappointment, and began work.

He settled down over the area and began painstakingly removing the added paint. It came off quite easily, being so distant in time, but as it came off he began to worry more and more. The signature was all gone, now, and there was nothing but blotches to replace it.

Strange lines and shapes, all in black-and-white, and not even in the same oils as the rest of the painting. He took a tiny sample of one and was about to take it to the lab for analysis, but decided against it for the moment.

With each tiny piece of black-and-white that appeared, Harvey's heart sank deeper and deeper. He'd given them his word, and he couldn't recover the added segment himself - even if he could, it wasn't exactly ethical.

When he got to the edge of the area, working as quickly as he could, he looked down at the whole he had created. It fitted with the rest, now. The picture around began to change texture from light to dark, and the strange area was just a continuation of that now. He knew this was the painting - this was what da Vinci, or whoever, had painted.

As he looked at it, he began to cry. Why was it not signed? What was it never signed? And why was the art community so stupid that they would not see it for the work of art it was without it having the signature on the bottom.

Harvey spent almost an hour with his head in his hands, and then went for a walk in the gallery. That usually cheered him up, not least because he was one of the few people trusted enough to be allowed into the gallery late at night. He could look at the paintings without the public being around to disturb him.

As he walked past, Harvery couldn't help but notice the signatures. Most were normal, but there were another three in their own collection with slightly odd dark areas in the bottom right corner. Harvery stopped and walked closer, staring intently at those areas.

He put a finger forwards to touch one, and then stopped himself. Even this late at night there were still alarms, and the security guards would do nothing for his mood.

First thing next morning he requested leave to examine two of the paintings from the gallery. As per normal this leave was granted.

He cut a minute piece of paint from the signature of each of them, and sent them to the lab, making sure they were marked as being from the painting he was supposed to be working on.

When they came back he almost despaired. He was just staring at the results when the directors walked in. As soon as they were inside they walked to either side of the door, the blotchy-faced one absent-mindedly looking at some sketches on the walls, while the other began looking at one of the paintings Harvery had borrowed.

The tall man, Mr Falworth, was holding copies of the lab reports. "What is the meaning of this?" he shouted, slamming them down on the desk.

Before anyone could reply, Louise burst in. Since the directors were standing to the sides, she didn't see them at first. "I did it!" she exclaimed.

Harvey was so surprised he couldn't think of anything to make the directors' presence obvious, so simply replied "What?"

"I can see these optowhatsits - the 3D things. They're marvellous, and really easy once you get the hang of them. You just let your eyes relax. Look at this one, it's... Oh." She turned and saw the directors, both looking at her, patiently waiting for her to finish. "Oh I'm sorry. I didn't..." Her faced turned bright red, and she sidled off into a corner.

"We repeat," said the tall man. "What is the meaning of this?"

"I was checking the signature again, just to confirm..."

"No, Mr McGann, you were checking the other paintings. Remember there's a security camera in this room, and we wondered why you wanted the other paintings. Are you telling us those are fakes too? That all the da Vinci's we have are fakes?"

"No, they aren't fakes. They're real."

The blotchy-faced man turned round and looked pointedly towards the painting. Louise was staring at it, intently studying it. She swore quietly, and began to speak. The blotchy-faced man interrupted her.

"Get that woman away from the painting. We've lost enough already without amateurs swanning in here. I don't know how you can work in this chaos!" He ran a hand along one of the desks, disturbing one of the heaps of papers and making some of it slide down onto the floor.

"Please, sir, I know this painting is genuine."

"So where's this signature you promised? It's just a mess! You think the great Leonardo would have left it like that?" he shouted, waving his hand over the painting.

Louise tried again to speak, but again the blotchy-faced man interrupted her. "Look, lady, if you haven't got any business here, I'd suggest you left. And if your boyfriend here doesn't have a damn good explanation for this he'll be going with you."

Louise pulled herself up to her full height and took a deep breath. Harvey hung his head, wondering what she was going to do to embarrass him. He was about to be fired, and she was about to make a scene. He wondered which felt worse.

"Are you saying that painting would be worthless without a signature?" she asked, surprisingly quietly.

"Yes," replied the tall man, evidently surprised that Louise was still in the room at all.

"But if there was a signature Harv wouldn't lose his job, and everything would be okay, right?"

The tall man nodded again.

Louise took a small piece of glass she'd picked up from the other side of the room, and placed it on the painting. "What's she..." began the blotchy-faced man. The tall man waved for him to be quiet.

"Come and look," Louise said to him, calm as anything.

He walked over and looked down. His jaw dropped, and he stood in total silence for almost a minute before he said a word.

"Oh my God!" His eyes were still wide as he looked up at Harvey again. "Well done, Harvey!" he exclaimed, slapping him on the shoulder. "And my sincere apologies."

"So I've still got my job?" asked Harvey, failing to understand what was going on.

"Of course. And a bonus to ensure you stay. You've made this museum rich."

Harvey walked over and looked down into the pane of glass. All he could see was the splodges below. Louise appeared beside him. As he looked at her reflection beside him, something else popped into existence.

Two letters, hanging in the space in front of him.

LV

A Last Secret

Twenty-six years ago they put a man on the moon. I remember this figure, because it was on the day I was born into a family of scientists. My father was, and still is, a prominent chemist who has tutored many students and, I am assured, advanced human understanding in his field. My mother was a mathematics teacher, although she left her job when she had her children. Both of my elder brothers moved into science, too. In my formative years I lived surrounded by a fascination with the world around us - an irresistible hunger to discover and learn. To conquer it, to explain it.

By way of contrast to my family, I gave up science at sixteen and went into the arts - a decision I could easily have had much reason to regret.

When I was young I was as keen to explore the world as my brothers, and we both studied and played together - for us it was the same thing. Our father left us questions to answer over the holidays, and we competed to understand them and discover their solutions.

As I grew I began to notice a change in my relationship with my brothers. They were still competing as vigorously as ever in the pursuit of knowledge, while I began turning to books - fantasy and science fiction mainly. My dreams stopped being of great discoveries and success, and became more and more of kings and wars and great nations. Imaginary places, where I went to watch. I always imagined myself like that. I understand some people imagine themselves as the kings, as the shapers of the land. My dreams showed all of this, like a film. Sometimes a scene would repeat until it worked better. That was my only style of nightmare, really - a scene repeating endlessly until it worked better. Sometimes I would see Robin Hood running through the forest and the sheriff's men would catch him. Then I would see it again, him getting just an inch or two further before they caught him again. And again. And again.

My brothers excelled, and I passed. I think that was mainly due to interest, but perhaps they were also better than me. I don't know. They went to university, and I followed along.

It was during my time there that I made my big break. The details are unimportant, but suffice it to say I earned myself a small fortune - more than I could ever spend, at least not on my lifestyle.

I bought myself a house in my second year, and rapidly realised how cut off I was becoming from the rest of the world. Not as if I wasn't talking to people, or wasn't getting out enough, but because no one really knew me. Not as I really was. I have a special room, you see.

One room, in the large house I own. Sometimes it's the basement, sometimes the attic, sometimes a secret room hidden away in one of the walls. Its exact location is immaterial. Its floor is covered with paper, reams and reams of notes I have made and thrown away, of letters written and never sent, and of letters received, read, and discarded.

In the centre of this room is my desk, a tiny island of wood floating on the sea of papers beneath. There is no chair, for I prefer to think and work standing up, and pace about a lot. I do no coherent work any more anyway - I just jot ideas down and give them to other people.

Just after this sea was formed, when I said good-bye to the floor for the last time, I noticed a piece of paper lying there that I did not recognise. Blue, two creases indicating it had been folded into thirds, and a slightly jagged corner as if ripped while being taken out of the envelope.

Obviously I leant down to pick it up.

About a inch away from it my hand stopped, and I got the strangest feeling. Like the times you're standing on the top of a tall building and lean forwards, or when driving just wonder what it would be like not to brake at this turn at all. An image of a possible future being discarded without thought, a path not being taken.

I stopped, and began to think about it, began to wonder what the paper said. That, in essence, was my mistake.

On blue paper there was very little it could be - a letter from someone. That was about it. But who? I did not remember the letter, and no one I knew had been in the room. So I began to wonder. I still don't understand why I didn't pick it up, but it seemed completely the wrong thing to do.

It was only the next day that I realised why.

The chances were, truth being told, that the letter was from my parents, or from my ex-girlfriend. Or from my current girlfriend for that matter. Whichever, it's impact on my life would be marginal to say the least. However, once I had picked it up, I would know this for sure. I could be absolutely certain that it was of no import.

As I sat looking at it I began to come up with more and more bizarre possibilities. This is an old house - perhaps it had been there all along and I hadn't noticed it before - perhaps it had fallen from a crack in the wall. Perhaps some supernatural creature put it there. Perhaps written on it, in suspicious red ink, would be a summoning for a foul demon - or the solution to mankind's problems. Or...

I leant forwards again, eager with anticipation. Again I got to within an inch of it and faltered. Again I felt the strange sensation - and imagined a butterfly flapping its wings in Tokyo. Stupid thing to think of, but there you go.

The more I thought about it, the more I felt I needed the piece of paper unread. My life had become dull - with my future secure and everything easy. I needed the mystery, maybe like my brothers needed their discovery.

But what if I didn't read it? I reasoned. Perhaps it was important.

How important could it be? If anyone had died, I would have been told by phone. If it was a detailed account of someone's love for me, surely they would tell me another way.

Then I began to get paranoid. What if it was my girlfriend telling me I had to understand how she felt or she was going to leave me?

There was a couple I knew at university who split up because of a lost letter. One slipped it under the other's door one night, telling her how he couldn't stand not knowing and had to find out if she loved him. If she didn't say anything the next day, the letter said, he would leave her.

Of course the cleaner found it and put it on the desk where it was found by the girl's admirer when he came round to see if she wanted to go out with him. He read it and dropped it into the bin. She never saw it.

I knew them both, you understand, before you accuse me of being the man in question. I lost my temper at him when I found out, which didn't help. I also told the poor unfortunate now-ex-boyfriend that she had never seen the letter, and that she never understood his sudden coldness towards her and felt shut out. That drove him damn near suicide. Fortunately we found him another girlfriend before he got too far down that road, and he is now happily married. At least he was last time we spoke. But I digress.

I have always thought that love was too important ever to place in one letter, and have repeated this belief to anyone who'd stick around long enough to listen. A letter can always be lost, however carefully it is delivered. A conversation cannot. Not that I'm the best person to ask about love, of course.

So anyway, ruling out the love letter concept, I began to wonder what could possibly be in the letter that I would regret not having read.

For three hours I sat there, and I could honestly think of no circumstance in which not reading the letter would harm me.

The reason I wanted to know was just to know, to discover. And when I had, I would be disappointed. This amazing feat of precognition was oddly enlightening.

I resolved not only to leave the paper for the day, but to leave it forever. Never once would I turn it over and read what it said, under any circumstances. To this end I slipped a piece of hardboard under it and a cheap piece of glass over it, and framed it.

I always felt it ought to have had a title, but I could never think of anything.

Every day I see it, and it has almost driven me mad sometimes, wondering. But I think it's good for me to have something like that in life. I wonder if some people have spouses for a similar reason. And I honestly hope that I will never weaken and take it down from my wall. I know I would be disappointed.

Recycling Tomorrow

The two geodesic hemispheres came slowly together, dwarfing the hedgehog which sat on a pedestal in the exact centre. It sniffed the air expectantly. The field generators locked into place around the sphere, all eighty-four of them pointing directly towards the creature. A tiny light at the end of each one lit up, registering its connection to the Taylor grid. The capacitors in the generators began charging. At that point the release became unstoppable.

One-third of a second before the capacitors discharged, filling the sphere with a pale blue glow, the hedgehog appeared in the receive-sphere. It sniffed the air once, looked towards its right side, and stopped breathing. Its nose stopped twitching, and it fell sideways off the pedestal.

"The Nobel prize presentation was the last public appearance Professor Taylor made before he was so brutally murdered by his own son, John Taylor, who is now being held in custody at Saint Augusta State Penitentiary. If convicted he is expected to face the death penalty under the new tough guidelines issued by Governor Pierras.

"The University community has been shocked by this senseless and motiveless killing of the man who, two years ago, single-handedly brought the world to the end of the age of the energy crisis and was exp..." Click.

Sarah tried to grab the remote. "Oy, I was watching that."

"I'm sick to death of it," replied Tony. "I've spent all bloody day on that story. Ed wants a motive, and he's determined that I'll find it."

"And so you will, love. I know you will. You're the best reporter they've got." She leant over to kiss him. He turned the telly back on and left the room. He couldn't stand her getting all sentimental.

"...a dog called Velvet was found in the coffin, only seconds before..."

Gary Webster, not for the first time that day, felt like picking up the largest textbook he could find and throwing it at Peter, his colleague and brother. He shut his eyes, and tried to ignore his brother's seemingly-endless supply of 'witty anecdotes', most of which he had heard many times over and didn't think were funny to begin with.

Peter, by way of contrast, was trying to lighten the mood, feeling that the two of them had got stuck in a rut since the last experiment went so badly wrong. Hell, Peter had said, what's a laboratory hedgehog between brothers? He hadn't convinced either of them.

The only thing that united both of them at that moment was a desire not to see the professor, the owner of said hedgehog, a previously happy little animal whose sole laboratory function was proving itself to respire by being placed in a glass jar once a year and emitting carbon-dioxide. This it had managed with consummate skill. Time-travel, however, it had been less capable of.

When the Professor Jackson arrived, the two immediately fell silent.

"So," said the professor, beaming. "How'd he do?"

Gary remained silent as long as he felt he could, hoping that Peter would find a way of telling the professor. Eventually, though, his nerve broke. "He did it. Reginald was the first animal to travel back in time."

"Was?"

When he saw Reginald, the professor began shouting, threw them both out of the lab and told them he never wanted to see them again. They both felt they'd escaped lightly.

Tony couldn't face another argument with Sarah, so he decided to go out for a drive. Running away, he knew, but he didn't need this kind of shit tonight. As always when he felt low, he unthinkingly threw himself back into his work, and within thirty minutes found himself just outside the fences surrounding the Taylor Energy Institute.

The superconducting cables overhead swayed gently in the breeze, appearing too calm to be carrying the entire electricity requirement of the planet. Tony stared towards the Institute itself, now overseen by the UN. It was so small. One building, in the centre of a huge complex whose sole function was to defend it. One reactor, set in motion and sealed forever. With Professor Taylor dead, no one even understood how it worked. They just used it, and with each passing year grew more and more dependent on the free and near-limitless electricity it seemed capable of providing.

Tony took out his notebook again, and looked down his jotted list of motives.

Greed. Money was an obvious factor. Taylor was rich. Not obscenely so, but he had made quite a nice nest-egg for himself. The problem was John didn't even try to escape. It was too stupid to be greed. None of the family were stupid.

Jealousy. He wanted to be the famous one? That didn't ring true, either.

Love was too absurd to consider, so he was left with temporary insanity. The most plausible he had, but still not good.

He closed the notebook again and sighed. An interview was out of the question - Taylor had already refused to be interviewed by all the major TV companies, so he was hardly likely to accept the offer from a minor newspaper.

Tony looked through the fence once more before driving away.

Neither Gary nor Peter felt up to joking when they got back to their experiments. Both of them had spent the intervening days wondering why they had failed. The autopsy on the hedgehog had ascertained that a small section of its nervous system had disappeared during transit. Without saying a word, both of them agreed to return to inanimate subject matter for the time being.

They returned almost to the beginning, back to the clock losing a millionth of a second. They calculated and recalculated the effects of certain quantities of power thrown into the grid. In every detail the experiments agreed with their predictions. A week passed in frustrating dead-ends, both of them failing to understand their failure.

Over lunch, as they were waiting in the queue for the jacket potatoes at the bar, Gary suddenly began staring. His jaw dropped.

"Something up?" asked Peter.

Gary just pointed, looking towards the microwave where the potatoes were being heated. "The potato rotates!" he exclaimed. Two of the girls in the queue looked at him like he was mad.

"Of course it does," said Peter, confused. "So you avoid getting cold spots. What's so...?" he began, and then realised what Gary was thinking.

Leaving their order, much to the anguish of the bar staff, the two ran back to the lab and checked the equipment. Sure enough, for a large object there was a slight increase in power at the centre of the sphere.

"So why did it disappear? Why didn't it just appear further back?" asked Peter.

"I don't know," replied Gary. He stared over at the sphere, trying to imagine the hedgehog inside it. He looked at the grid generators positioned around the edge, all pointing towards the dead centre. "Maybe the hotspot in the centre is more localised. Maybe that power is even more concentrated and we threw a tiny speck back a larger time difference?"

"But we know the size of the missing nervous system. The hotspot has to be that size."

"Unless," said Gary, peering closer towards the box, "a reaction took place that dragged the surrounding material with the central section." His eyes were wide-open as the thoughts began snowballing through his head, almost failing to articulate themselves. "And the clock wasn't affected because it has a gap in the centre, so nothing got ripped out."

Peter thought for a moment, and then nodded. "So how do we test that then?"

"We find out how much energy this thing generated and precisely where the hotspot is. Then we send something solid through and see what happens."

Tony found himself in a bar by himself, not drinking. He knew that once he started he would get totally out of his head. However, he still wanted to be near alcohol for when the possibility of being drunk became more appealing.

The only person who understood was John Taylor, so he was the only way Tony was ever going to crack the case.

With an enormous effort of will, Tony stood up and walked back out the bar. He got back in his car and drove to Saint Augusta. It was the only place he'd find any answers. Even if it was the middle of the night.

By the time he reached a hill-top overlooking the prison it had started pouring with rain. Tony took out his long-distance lens so he could look through the perimeter fence. There was a small police van parked just outside the main prison building, its engine still on although its lights weren't. Tony increased the magnification. It had a driver inside, and three civilians behind the back doors, milling about waiting for something.

Tony quickly looked to the side, and almost dropped the lens as he saw John Taylor being manhandled towards and into the waiting vehicle. The three men next to the doors looked around nervously, then slammed the doors shut. One of them ran round to the front and got in, while the other two turned and walked back into the prison building.

As the van pulled away, its lights remained off. The gates opened and it drove out onto the main highway. After another thirty seconds its lights turned on. Tony took one glance back at the prison, then turned his car round and began driving back down towards the highway. On the way down he fumbled with a route map he had stashed in the glove compartment, trying to work out where the van would be going, so he could follow with more subtlety.

After a very tense twenty minutes, the van pulled up outside a wooden shack in the middle of nowhere. Tony parked his car in some trees a couple of hundred yards away and walked, slowly and carefully, towards it. As he reached the shack, the van was already driving off. The lights inside the shack were on.

Tony crept up to the wall and tried to hear what was being said inside. His footsteps and breathing sounded so loud he could hardly believe no one heard him. There was the crackle of a fire inside the shack, and two voices. He pressed his ear up against the cold and wet wall of the shack to hear.

"Now, Mr Taylor," said a deep male voice. "We have kept our side of the bargain. I think it's time for you to start talking."

"All right." The second voice, younger than the first. "My father's papers are in locker 1061 in the main University concourse."

"Well, that was painless, wasn't it?"

There was a single gunshot, and a low thud. Without thinking, Tony turned and sprinted back to his car. When he reached it, he started it and raced as fast as it would go towards the University.

Almost two months of careful calculations later, Gary was no nearer to working out what was going on, and Peter's experiments had produced conflicting results. Depending on the size of the object and how much power was thrown into it, sometimes it travelled a tiny amount back in time, up to about half-a-second, and sometimes it disappeared altogether.

When they sat down to review their progress, there were only two experiments remaining. One, to receive something back in time and then not send it, in an attempt to create a temporal paradox. Or two, to send one of them back to find out where the disappearing items were going.

As in most things, they came down on opposite sides. Gary was in favour of the paradox approach, while Peter thought that was pointless. "What," he argued, "would it tell us? It *has* to be impossible."

"Why? If we begin the experiment and then don't carry it out once it's finished, what would be the problem with that?"

"I'm sure it's impossible," he replied, not feeling quite up to having this discussion again. They had spent so long discussing time travel, including of course its theoretical impossibility, that they had long-since exhausted the topic. They still did not agree, however.

"Well there won't be any harm in trying then, will there?"

Peter had to concede that point, and the two of them set about preparing the experiment. Right on cue, the clock appeared, one-quarter of a second before it was supposed to be sent. Its weight triggered a computer instruction to abort the experiment. Following that, neither had a very good idea of what happened.

Gary woke first, and found Peter still dazed. After a drink of water and almost an hour to recover, they rewound the laboratory tape to find out what had happened.

Pulling up the video window, they watched in silence as the experiment began. They remembered it accurately, right up to the point when the computer was supposed to abort the experiment. At that moment a giant spark arced across the video image. Neither could see where it came from, but when it had faded again they saw themselves lying unconscious on the floor.

"So," said Peter, after stopping the tape. "Time protects itself..."

"So we make it the other way round," replied Gary, obviously angry. "The jump can only happen if a switch stays held together, and the weight breaks the connection. Anything like that and it doesn't happen," he said, indicating the screen.

Again the two tried, and again the experiment finished successfully, this time with the switch simply failing to break under the weight.

Peter couldn't help but laugh.

Three more times they tried, and three more times events conspired to keep the experiment going. When finally Gary could think of nothing else to try, he turned to Peter, a flash of hate in his eyes. "Okay, then. You've got your way. Let's try it."

"What?" asked Peter, frightened of his brother's sudden mood-swing.

"Send me back."

"What? You said it was too dangerous."

"Well I've changed my mind. There's got to be some point to this bloody thing," he said, bashing his hand into one of the generators.

"No. You'll just die. That won't solve anything."

"I won't just die," said Gary, mimicking his brother's voice. "I'll find out where everything else goes when we send too much energy through it."

"You want to disappear?"

"I'll find out. That's what counts. I have to know."

"No. I can't."

Gary turned on his brother, grabbing his shoulders and shaking him. "You've got to, Peter. I have to know. And if you don't, I'll do it myself."

"That would be suicide."

"Then suicide it is. Let me go. It's my life."

Peter thought for a few minutes, and then refused. "Sorry, Gary," he said, and walked out. "I'll think about it again when you've calmed down."

Five minutes after Peter left the lab, the lights suddenly went dim. Peter understood instantly, but still didn't go back to the lab until the police came to question him. He already knew he would never see his brother again.

Tony ran along the concourse, his legs burning hot just as his lungs were frozen from the cold air he was forcing into them as he ran. He began counting down to the correct locker as he ran, uncertain how he was going to open it when he got there.

At 1090 he tripped and slid the rest of the way to 1061.

His fingers felt the outside of the plastic locker, pushing themselves into every tiny scratch, wondering what it contained. He pulled at the door, but it didn't budge. He cursed and took out his keys. The largest key he possessed was his car-key, so he stuck that in as far as it would go and pushed.

Nothing.

He looked sideways to see if there was anyone about. Fortunately no one seemed to be in the building at this time of the morning. He turned back to the key and pushed again, but it still didn't budge.

He cursed, almost bursting into tears. So close, and only a tiny bit of plastic stood between him and the knowledge. The greatest story of the decade.

A car pulled up outside. He heard its tyres screech to a halt, and then heard its engine keep running. He knew it was *them*, whoever *they* were.

His lungs fluttered as he gasped for breath, realising he only had a few moments more before the men would see him. They had already killed once for this. With a desperation fuelled entirely by fear, he turned away and kicked the key harder than he thought possible. When he brought his foot away he saw that the key had pushed almost through the sole of his shoe. He pulled it out, trying to ignore the burning pain in his ankle.

He looked at the locker. It was swinging open. Inside was a single cardboard file.

Without thinking any more, Tony grabbed the file and began running.

Before he reached the end of the concourse he heard them. One of them shouted, and they broke into a run. His lungs became louder after that, and although he knew they were there, he could not hear them any more.

As he ran towards a window next to the staircase at the end of a second corridor, he realised he wasn't going to outrun them. Tony held his breath. He shut his eyes, and jumped. The window shattered around him.

When he opened his eyes, he was lying on gravel, aching from head to toe. It was cold and dark, and he felt damp. He pulled himself to his feet and looked around. Everything was dark and silent. Nothing seemed to move anywhere, but Tony knew it was only a matter of time. He half-slid, half-ran down a grassy bank, and found his car.

Once inside he felt slightly safer, although much worse.

He drove as far as he could before he felt so faint he feared passing out, and then he pulled off the road and turned on the car's internal light.

Flicking the file open, he began to read. The further he got, the more engrossed he became. He never heard the car pull up a few yards away, and did not hear the men until they pulled the door open and stuck a gun to his head.

"Out of the car! Now!"

He did as he was told. As he stood up he felt even more faint, and almost slipped. Another man moved past him and grabbed the file from the front seat.

"Do you know what it says?" asked Tony.

"Nope."

"Do you know how the energy-grid works?"

"Nope," said his captor, still completely uninterested.

"Killing," he said, and then realised what the gun pointing at him meant. He looked down at it, and realised he didn't care. A shiver ran down his spine, and he pulled himself up so he was standing straight. "Taylor found a way to enable time travel back to here, using that reactor. Or rather, into that reactor. So all the best minds of the future, every one of them who tries to send things back in time, will fail. All the energy they send back goes into the grid." He paused for a moment. "I'm right, aren't I?" He didn't understand why, but knowing if he was right still felt important.

The man holding the gun smiled. "I don't know, and I don't care, either." He raised the gun so it was level with Tony's heart. "You're not going to tell anyone."

"Obviously," said Tony quietly, looking over towards the road. "Those street-lights are connected to the energy-grid, and they're still on."

Turing to the Death

The phone rang at precisely twelve-noon.

Rob went to answer it approximately eight seconds later, after spending two seconds wondering whether it was the phone or the doorbell. He resolved for the third time that week to get the doorbell changed.

Twelve seconds after noon, Rob picked the phone up and said hello.

"Doctor Robert Martin," said an electronic voice at the other end of the line.

Rob assumed it was a question, and replied accordingly: "speaking."

"My name is Boris. I do not believe you have heard of me."

"Right. It's Haydyn, is it?" asked Rob, trying not to burst into hysterics. Boris indeed.

"No. My name is Boris."

"Alistair. You finally bought the CD-ROM drive then? Excellent. We can have that game of two-player *Wing Commander V*."

"No, Doctor Martin. My name is Boris."

Rob took the phone away from his ear and looked at it before realising how stupid it would have looked. "What, really?" he asked, confused. An electronic voice called Boris? It didn't seem possible it was serious. "I suppose you're from the Russian Union, then, are you?"

"No, Doctor Martin. I am not from anywhere." There was still no tone, no emphasis. This was not a voice-distorter, then. This was the real thing. Someone typing into a computer somewhere. "I was built in New Mexico. I am what you call an artificial intelligence."

"Oh, for heaven's sake," said Rob in an exhausted tone before putting the phone down. Double glazing salesmen and newspapers doing surveys were bad enough, but people ringing up pretending to be computers...?

The air conditioning units turned up by one-percent as the processors increased their clock-cycle once more. Gary watched on in wonder as Boris churned through another of the problems its creators had given it - this time to produce a correct and working proof of Fermat's last theorem. Boris had got the proof down to eight pages of normally printed paper, but for some reason had continually printed it out on one page with a tiny font. Every time Gary had asked it why, Boris had replied "One page is better than eight."

As Gary had drunk his fourth cup of hot chocolate, wondering whether this time the powder would be mixed in properly or not, he had found himself wondering whether Boris was printing on one page out of efficiency or out of a desire to look impressive.

When he stopped to think about it, he laughed. Boris wasn't created to have a personality, he was created to solve problems.

Problems, problems and more problems. His entire *raison d'être*. No, it's entire *raison d'être*. Gary had been accused once of empathising with his programs. It seemed odd, now, given their line of research, that it was still the subject of even mild disapproval.

A light flashed on the terminal in front of him. Gary pulled his feet off the desk and sat up straight. The boss had opened the security-door and wanted his usual report. Gary leaned over and pulled the windows shut. He preferred the air, but there was a balcony running the length of the computer science building, and security liked the windows to stay shut.

"Morning Gary," said Professor John Hutchins as he opened the door. John always wore a grey suit and an old school tie. It was obvious he had a mild disapproval of Gary's T-shirt and jeans, but he never said anything.

"John."

"So how's our patient?" John always made the same joke, every day. It seemed impolite not to laugh at it, so Gary forced a smile.

"Well as ever. He... It's begun contacting bulletin boards on its own, now."

"Where? And what's it doing there?" asked John, pulling out a chair and sitting down. He looked concerned, like a father hearing about his son's exploits. Gary smiled again and tried to put the metaphor out of his head.

"It got through to the Federal Library Service to look up some background for the problems we gave it." Gary looked down at his notes and flicked back a page. He began running his finger down it. "Oh yes, I opened a link to the University Bulletin board debating pages to give it some language practice - it did brilliantly, by the way."

"Does it understand, though?" asked John, leaning forwards to look at the notes. Gary found himself sitting up straighter to avoid John seeing.

"Seems to. It could repeat and paraphrase without difficulty. Still has occasional problems with over-analysing. It found eighteen underlying pieces of symbolism in a rude limerick this afternoon." Gary had the limerick jotted down and hoped John wouldn't ask for it. He had been in hysterics as Boris had explained it's meaning.

John smiled approvingly. "Anything else?"

"Oh, yes. One other phone call to a bulletin board I don't know. Didn't seem to connect, though, as the line speed kept changing radically. It was only connected for a few seconds."

"When was that."

"Four a.m."

"Odd. What was the number?"

"Overseas. I already checked - it's in England."

"Where did it get the number from?"

"I don't know, to be honest. When I find out, you'll be the first to know."

At six o'clock precisely the phone rang again.

Again Rob ran to it and picked it up.

Again the electronic voice sounded. "Doctor Martin. Please do not hang up the phone."

Rob sat down with a sigh. "You again. Are you still an artificial intelligence?"

"Yes."

Rob shook his head and hung up.

Before he had even stood up again, the phone rang.

"Hello Boris," he said as he picked up the phone.

There was a pause. For an instant he thought it must be someone else. The estate agents about the house? Perhaps he should hang up again and pretend they got the wrong number?

"Hello Doctor Martin." The electronic voice again. Boris.

"What do you want?"

"I just want to talk to you. Please do not hang up. I am interested in your ideas."

Rob remembered the article he had posted to the net the week before, attacking a professor in New Mexico for his researches into AI. He nodded as he understood. "New Mexico, you said?"

"Yes."

"Professor Phoenix?"

"You imply that I am Professor Ray Phoenix."

"But of course you're Boris. Sorry, I forget."

"Correct. I am Boris. Are you willing to talk to me."

Of course sarcasm would be lost on him - he was American.
"Okay, you win. I'm listening. What do you want to discuss?"

"Me. You say I cannot exist."

"If you are still claiming to be an artificial intelligence then
yes, I claim you are impossible."

"Why."

"Because, as I said in my article, computers can only be
programmed to do what a person knows how he does, and we
do not know how we think, therefore we cannot create a
machine which can do it for us."

"Doctor Martin, you are speaking to one."

"A computer?"

"Yes. If you wish proof, ask me a mathematical question."

"That would only prove you have a calculator handy."

"Not if I answer instantly."

"That would prove a good speech recognition system, which I
also accept as being possible, at least as far as numbers. Since
you are speaking through your computer, you could easily
enough switch... Hang on." Rob looked away and thought for
a moment. "Hang on, I need a piece of paper." He grabbed the
back of an envelope and scribbled down a multiplication: 585.4
* 2034.22. He punched it into his own calculator, and got the
answer ready.

"Right, he began. Are you ready?"

"I am."

"Point 4 on top of the number 85 with a 5 on the front, multiplied by a six digit number, 4 digits before and 2 after the decimal point, all of them 2's except for the 3 before the decimal point with are 0, 3 and 4."

Without hesitation the reply came back: 1,188,897.168.

"That's impressive, Boris, however you did it. You've got my attention, although still not my belief."

"What would it take to make you believe I am not a person."

"That's easy. If you are separated from any external influence and don't contain a human being, then I would believe that what you have said emanated from a computer."

"Then come and see me, and you will believe."

"Ah, no, Boris. That doesn't mean you are intelligent. You may be a computer, but I had a long conversation with Elijah years ago which was quite impressively convincing. If you have been programmed to talk to me, then I could well believe that this is still just impressive prediction and psychology coupled with a healthy dose of good program. But I don't believe you are even a computer, so it's largely irrelevant."

The phone clicked. Rob put the phone down and leant back, wondering. Could it really...? No, of course not. It was impossible.

"Thanks for coming, John," said Gary, clicking up his window of information.

"What is it? It'd better be important or my wife's going to hit the roof."

"Boris called England again, so I checked the directory to find out who he was calling."

"Who? You mean it was a person?"

"That's right. A man called Robert Martin from London, England. I found out he posted an article on the University bulletin board a few days ago, arguing against Professor Phoenix's research, saying that AI was impossible."

John laughed. "Ironic. Why did Boris call him?"

"I don't know. He won't say."

John's eyes lit up, his face instantly turning serious. "What do you mean he won't say. It called someone, presumably spoke to him, and won't say why? Find out!"

"I can't, John," replied Gary, feeling increasingly nervous. A lot of the support software had been his, and he was embarrassed to have to admit the fault with it. "The audit didn't cover speech, just data. The compression software couldn't do much with it, and the log was growing too quickly, so it was left out. We don't know what he said."

"But you've got the number, right?"

"Yes."

"So call this Robert Martin of London, England, and find out what he said. In fact, give me the number and I'll try to get him over here. We may be talking sabotage, you know. Do you know if this guy has any way of profiting by our failure?"

"He's a computer scientist at Imperial College, London. That's it."

"Right, leave it to me. I'll find out what they've been talking about."

At sixteen minutes and twenty-three seconds past seven o'clock, the phone rang.

Rob felt slightly relieved. If it wasn't exactly on the hour, it wasn't Boris.

"Hello?" he said.

"Robert Martin?" asked an American voice.

"Speaking. Who is this please?"

"My name is John Hutchins."

"Do I know you?" asked Rob, wondering if this was another weird phone call after all.

"I don't believe so. You do, I think, know one of my colleagues. Professor Phoenix."

"Oh yes, the artificial intelligence man. He hasn't replied to my last post yet. Is there something wrong?"

"Not at all. It's just he would like to meet you and discuss the future of his research with you. He has a project running at the moment. I believe you are aware of it already." Rob smiled as it all began to make sense.

"You mean Boris?"

"Yes. What do you think?"

"I would be intrigued to see how it's done, certainly." And if the Professor could be convinced to turn his not-inconsiderable talents towards achievable goals, all the better.

"We are arranging with our funding body to pay for your flight and accommodation if you could spare us a couple of days."

"When?"

"You could fly out from London overnight tomorrow, and we could arrange the meeting for Monday morning."

"I don't know - I'll have to check."

"Check all you like, as long as you're on that flight."

"I suppose they'll manage without me. Fine. Could you fax me through the details."

"Give me five minutes."

Rob hated flying. On the first plane he sat next to a stereotypical yuppie, Phil, and his surprisingly pleasant wife, Anne. How she could put up with him was beyond Rob, but he was glad of someone to talk to, and tried his best to keep the conversation away from politics. When Phil finally decided to have a nap, Rob took out his portable chess computer and concentrated on a game, trying as hard as he could to forget that he was in two-hundred tons of steel hanging in the air.

On the second, far smaller, plane, Rob thought for some time he was going to have a double-seat to himself. Just before the plane began taxiing away, however, a frail old man in a black suit parked himself on the seat and promptly began snoring loudly. Rob stared out of the window as the plane moved away from the terminal, taking deep breaths. Truth was, he didn't just hate flying. People weren't too good either.

When he finally left the last plane of the day and walked out into the arrivals area he felt like dropping to his knees and kissing the ground. Only then people would have thought he was the Pope.

Professor Hutchins was waiting for him. Rob eyed up the professor. His first reaction was of a harmless middle-aged man, the kind one expected in an academic institution. The only parts of his face that seemed alive were his eyes, which Rob noticed were looking him over in an equally fervent manner.

"Thank you for coming, Robert," said Hutchins, looking away as he spoke. "Your time is much appreciated."

"How could I miss an opportunity to meet Boris?"

Hutchins smiled a slightly unnerving smile, and led Rob away. They got into a car waiting outside the airport, and stopped off briefly at a hotel to check in before driving off again.

They drove onto a university campus, with its traditional array of students milling about carrying piles of books clenched to their chests. They drove slowly through a crowd milling slowly across the road, and then passed through a set of security gates. At that point Rob began to feel nervous, partly because of the security gates themselves, but partly because a gentle rain had begun which made it harder for Rob to get a coherent idea of where he was going.

"Where are we?"

"Boris's house," said Hutchins in a voice that suggested he didn't want to answer any questions just yet.

The car stopped, and Hutchins got out and put up an umbrella. Rob assumed he was meant to follow, so he got out, too. Hutchins moved the umbrella so it didn't quite cover either of them properly - presumably not his intention.

"Follow me, please," said Hutchins. Rob was beginning to dislike the man's tone. He had come here of his own accord, after all, and felt he could expect a certain amount of politeness.

Rob stopped walking. "Where are we going?" he said, aware of how stupid he would look, standing in the rain acting in such a childish manner.

"Do you want to meet Boris or not?"

Rob nodded, sighed, and followed Hutchins as he entered the building.

They walked along seven corridors, passed two hot drinks machines, one cold drinks machine and two snack machines and then took the fourth door on the right. Hutchins motioned Rob inside, saying "If you wouldn't mind waiting here, I'll go and check whether everything's ready for you."

Feeling he had little choice, Rob sat down and made himself comfortable.

A second later, Hutchins popped his head round the door again.

"Feel free to help yourself to coffee. There's a machine in the corner."

Rob looked over the line of chairs and saw a pot of coffee, already made. He poured it, searched around for some cartons of milk. He drank the first mug in under a minute, the warmth being very comforting after the rain, and the caffeine helping to fight off the impending exhaustion from the flight. The second mug was slower, interrupted by speculations as to what was so important that it should warrant such frantic activity.

Gary looked up as John entered. "He's here," said John.

"Good. Boris wants to see him."

"What?"

"Boris just finished dialling up the airport computer. It seems he found another problem to solve in the password system the airport uses. He hacked his way in and found out that Dr Martin is coming here. He wants to see him."

John slammed his fist on the desk. "For the last time, Gary, 'he' is an 'it', and it has just committed a federal offence. I don't think you should be laughing!"

Gary sat up straight and looked down at the floor. "Sorry, John."

"Do you know what it wants to talk about?"

"It said it wants to discuss its existence with someone who denies it."

John smiled, holding back a laugh. "Curiouser and curiouser."

Professor Hutchins returned a few minutes later. "Boris wants to speak to you."

Rob suddenly perked up. "Does he?"

"It."

"Does it."

"I would like to impose a condition, though."

"What's that?"

"After you've spoken, you tell me what you said when it phoned you on Saturday."

"Fair enough."

Rob was led to a small and extremely cold room. There were stacks of computers making an inner wall, almost defensively around a central desk covered with monitors and keyboards. Outside this wall was a mess of cables, most going up towards the myriad power points, but some disappearing into floor or ceiling. There was an incredibly loud humming noise, not unlike the sound of a plane's engines. Rob walked into what would be the courtyard of the castle and sat down next to a screen which had a small sticker saying "BORIS" stuck to it. Hutchins followed him in and sat down behind him. A few moments later another man in jeans and a T-shirt walked in.

"My connection's gone dead," he said.

A monitor in the corner was flashing up that there were no

external connections.

The centre of the screen cleared, and some words appeared. *Is that enough proof?*

Rob began typing. *Yes. That you are a computer.*

Then am I an artificial intelligence.

That depends on whether you are intelligent or not.

So how do you propose to determine?

Can you convince aardvark me?

Rob leant back. The screen paused. The scruffier of the two men moved uncomfortably in his chair.

I think I probably buffalo can.

Both men behind laughed. Rob turned to them and smiled. "A sense of humour, eh?"

How now brown cow?

Is this not enough?

What do you think about treacle? he typed, as quickly as he could.

It is sticky. What is there to think?

Too standard. Originality?

What about it? I proved Fermat's last theorem. The proof was original.

That is mathematics. That is not intelligence.

So what is?

Originality, expression, ingenuity.

Which I possess.

No. You have been programmed. Very well, but still programmed.

Then you define intelligence as what I have not got.

Rob looked down for a few moments, and felt slightly sad. It was true. And he stuck to the principle. He could not prove that this machine was not intelligent, but he still did not believe it was. *True*, he typed, and then turned away and stood up.

Hutchins looked at the other man for a moment, and then they both looked at Rob.

"So," Rob began. "Who programmed it to try to prove itself to me?"

They looked at each other again. "We didn't. It must have wanted to."

Rob turned back to it. The words had faded from the screen, replaced by the words "To be or not to be..."

The lights flickered for a few second, then the screen went black.

"Oh my God," said Hutchins. "What's happened?"

The other man pushed Rob to one side and began typing furiously on the keyboard. "It's shut itself down!"

"Can it recover?"

"Not back to the level it was at. It's a dynamic entity."

They both looked at Rob. He couldn't think of anything to say but "sorry."

"Well are you convinced?" asked the professor. "He seems to have died trying to convince you!"

Rob looked at the panic and anger on the faces of the two men.

Then he nodded. "Yes. All right. I am convinced."

Only then did he look back at the screen. In the top-left, in small type, were the words "Are you convinced?"

Notes and Explanations

This collection of stories was written while I was part of an amateur writers' group in Coventry in 1995. I am grateful to them for their encouragement, so thanks to Andrew (who went on to be best man at my wedding), Keith (who still meets up and drinks with me every St Patrick's day), Alison, Nick and Alastair.

Inspiration was one of several stories the group wrote inspired by the REM video for Everybody Hurts. Mine is a bit more tangentially related to it, and the biggest argument it caused was whether Bolero really sounded like a train. I still think it does.

King Arthur, Samantha, and Batman was written after I repeatedly failed to ask out a pretty girl at work called Samantha. I suppose I have her to thank for never giving me the time of day – otherwise I'd never have written this story.

www.ingramcontent.com/pod-product-compliance
Lightning Source LLC
Chambersburg PA
CBHW051300170626
46809CB00004B/1740